I0834297
Deep
Delve to the
Darkness
BOOK 1 - THE GLASS VANGUARD
NICHOLAS SCHMIT

Deep Delve to the Darkness

The Glass Vanguard

Nicholas Schmit

Book 1

Formatted using Lacuna

Deep
Delve to the
Darkness
BOOK 1 - THE GLASS VANGUARD
NICHOLAS SCHMIT

Deep Delve to the Darkness
Book 1
The Glass Vanguard

Nicholas Schmit
SchmitHouse Games LLC

Publication Date 4/7/2026

Prologue

The Official Archives of the High Keep

The island of Orowait is a realm woven from miracles and resilience, a sanctuary entirely encircled by relentless, churning waves. Mariners speak in hushed, terrified tones of the monstrous shadows lurking beyond the horizon, but within the city's towering stone walls, a golden era of peace has reigned for a millennium.

But our peace was hard-won.

Long ago, a fiery comet streaked across the heavens, striking the absolute heart of Orowait. A suffocating veil of pitch-black darkness swallowed the city, leaving behind a yawning crater nearly a mile across. The bravest of our ancestors built a massive wooden lift, discovering the subterranean realm of "Layer"—a terrifying frontier of endless golden plains and lurking nightmares. To protect the surface, the High Council founded the four noble academies: the Explorer to lead, the Medic to heal, the Watcher to guard, and the Orator to chronicle.

Yet, it was not the academies alone that saved us. It was the First.

On the 550th anniversary of the meteor's fall, a blinding blue light descended from the heavens. Paldyne, the island's only Hero to master all four disciplines, raced to the highest peak and caught the falling star. It was a girl with hair as pale as moonlight—Melmori, a Princess of the Sky.

When the monsters surged from the well in a cataclysmic tremor, Paldyne and Melmori did not hesitate. Together, the Hero and the

Princess descended into the abyss to confront the nightmare. For three long years, the city wept, fearing the dark had claimed them.

But the Light always prevails.

Three years later, the great iron lift groaned to life, bringing our champions back to the sun. They returned triumphant, having sealed the Gate at the bottom of the world forever. Melmori chose to remain bound to the earth, and together they ruled with wisdom, raising their miracle daughter, Reverie, and cementing a thousand-year golden age before passing peacefully into the Light.

This is the history every child of Orowait is taught. It is a beautiful, flawless, and comforting legacy. It is the absolute, unquestionable truth of the High Council.

Generations later, the bloodline of Reverie spread through the island, gifting her descendants with mysterious, latent abilities. On the day of his graduation, a young man named Marche was chosen to lead a new era of exploration. Accompanied by his childhood friends—Leo, Anna, and Teitra—Marche stepped onto the heavy wooden planks of the lift.

He looked down into the dark, his heart swelling with pride. He carried the suffocating, perfect weight of the First Hero's legacy on his broad shoulders, completely ready to follow in the footsteps of gods.

He had absolutely no idea he was stepping into a graveyard.

CHAPTER 1
The Endless Plains

The ancient elevator groaned as it descended deep into the well, carrying four destined souls into the heart of Layer. The air grew incredibly thick with anticipation, transforming each breath into a silent prayer to the unknown. When the heavy iron doors finally slid open, a radiant golden light spilled forth, revealing a breathtaking world seemingly untouched by time. Before them lay the Endless Plains—an infinite, sprawling expanse of rolling grass kissed by an eternal sun frozen high in a flawless blue sky. The tall grass swayed gently in a warm breeze, whispering the forgotten secrets of ages past.

Marche stepped off the platform first. He was tall, with tousled brown hair and piercing blue eyes. His outwardly calm demeanor expertly belied the fierce fire burning within—he was a restless explorer whose mind often wandered far beyond the visible horizon. His gaze swept over the endless fields with profound awe, his heart racing at the sheer promise of discovery.

Beside him, Anna moved with an effortless grace and purpose. Her striking blonde hair caught the brilliant sunlight, and her vivid red eyes shone with an insatiable, consuming curiosity. She yearned to see, to learn, and to understand every single corner of this strange new world. To her, every rustle in the grass was a profound mystery beckoning her forward.

Leo followed, stoic and intensely focused. His green hair framed sharp, analytical features, and his intense yellow eyes reflected a mind utterly consumed by science and medicine. Obsessed with understanding the unknown, he often forgot the physical world around him entirely, lost deeply in thought about toxins, remedies, and anatomy.

Teitra brought up the rear, her fiery red hair providing a vivid, striking contrast against the golden plains. Her golden eyes gleamed with both intelligence and an innate warmth. As a master of languages—fluent in the tongues of humans and monsters alike—she possessed the unique ability to listen not only to words, but to the subtle tones and rhythms that revealed hidden truths. Her voice was the crucial bridge between vastly different worlds.

Teitra held a brass compass steady in her hand. "The gate lies due east," she said softly, her voice carrying a comforting confidence and calm.

Marche smiled, a spark of pure excitement lighting up his blue eyes. "Then east it is. Let's see what secrets this world holds".

Anna's eyes gleamed as she stepped forward eagerly, her sense of wonder uncontained. "Every blade of grass, every shadow—there's so much to uncover".

Leo adjusted his heavy pack, his mind already meticulously cataloging the surrounding flora and fauna. "Stay alert," he warned. "The plains may look peaceful, but there's danger in every corner".

Together, the four of them moved out into the vast sea of grass, the long blades whispering softly beneath their boots. The sun's unyielding light cast long, dramatic shadows across the earth, and the wind carried their silent, shared vow: to uncover the mysteries of Layer, to protect their home, and to become legends. The Endless Plains welcomed them, vast and eternal, as their terrifying and beautiful journey into the unknown truly began.

As they marched, the tense atmosphere was occasionally broken by the comfortable banter of lifelong friends.

Teitra flashed a bright grin. "Leo, you do realize that 'left' and 'right' aren't just suggestions, right? Especially when we're being followed by those creepy shadow things".

Leo laughed, his yellow eyes scanning the horizon. "Hey, I'm just making sure we don't miss any cool spots. You never know when a hidden treasure or a monster might pop up".

"Or when we might accidentally walk off the wrong way because you ignored my directions," Teitra teased lightly.

Leo simply shrugged. "I prefer to think of it as 'creative exploration.' Besides, you always save me when I mess up".

Teitra offered a soft, quiet smile. "Yeah, I guess I do. Maybe if you paid a little more attention to me, you wouldn't get lost so often".

Completely oblivious to the deeper meaning in her words, Leo gestured to his hands. "Oh, I'm definitely paying attention... mostly to the map. But hey, you're a great navigator".

Teitra playfully nudged him in the ribs. "Maybe one day you'll pay attention to me for more than just directions".

Leo laughed again. "Teitra, you're impossible. But honestly, I wouldn't want anyone else by my side".

At that, Teitra's heart quietly fluttered against her ribs. "Good," she murmured. "Because I'm not going anywhere".

Walking a few paces ahead, Anna glanced over her shoulder at Leo, who was already completely absorbed in examining a peculiar plant, muttering rapid scientific notes under his breath. She nudged Marche softly, a teasing smile playing on her lips.

"You ever notice how Leo's so focused on his science stuff, he doesn't even realize Teitra's practically hanging on his every word?" Anna observed.

Marche chuckled, adjusting his pack strap nervously as he stole a glance at Teitra, who was subtly watching Leo with an unmistakable sparkle in her golden eyes. "Yeah, it's like he's got blinders on. He's completely oblivious. You'd think after all these years, he'd catch on".

Anna laughed quietly, a faint tint of pink rushing to her cheeks. "Makes you wonder if some people are just naturally clueless... or maybe it's easier to ignore what's right in front of you".

Marche's gaze met hers for a brief, heavily charged moment, and his voice softened considerably. "Maybe. Or maybe some things are just harder to say than others".

Anna's smile faltered for a heartbeat under the weight of his gaze, and she quickly changed the subject to break the tension. "Well, at least Leo's dedication means Teitra's got someone to care about, even if he doesn't know it yet".

Marche nodded, a warm, comforting feeling settling deep in his chest. "Yeah. And maybe one day, we'll figure out how to say what we're both too scared to admit". They shared a quiet, knowing laugh, the unspoken feelings between them hanging gently in the warm air as they continued their trek through the endless plains.

Their peaceful dynamic was abruptly tested when a sudden, swirling dust cloud began rising ominously on the horizon.

"Storm coming. We need shelter—now," Anna commanded.

"There! Those rocks up ahead. Quick!" Marche pointed. They sprinted toward a cluster of large boulders, huddling defensively behind the rocky outcrop just as the dust storm swept violently over the plains. The wind howled mercilessly, carrying sharp grit that stung their skin and threatened to fill their lungs.

Leo coughed, pulling his gear tight. "Keep your masks on. This dust could cause respiratory issues".

Beside him, Teitra closed her eyes, chanting softly to keep them grounded. "The storm is fierce, but it will pass. Stay calm".

When the howling wind finally subsided, the plains somehow seemed even more vast and deeply mysterious. As they resumed their journey, Anna spotted subtle movement near a distant thicket.

"Something's there. Could be a predator—or another explorer," she warned.

"Let's approach cautiously," Marche instructed. They moved quietly, weapons drawn and ready. To their profound relief, emerging from the tall grass was merely a small herd of plainsrunners—graceful, deer-like creatures with tawny coats that blended perfectly with the golden grass.

Teitra smiled at the serene sight. "A peaceful encounter. Layer is full of surprises".

Leo immediately knelt into the dirt to examine the ground. "Their tracks could tell us about the local ecosystem. We should document this".

As the eternal sun cast long, unchanging shadows across the plains, mimicking a dusk that would never truly come, the team found a natural clearing surrounded by vibrant wildflowers to set up their camp. Gathered around a small fire, they shared stories and future plans.

"This place is beautiful, but we can't forget why we're here. The gate awaits," Marche reminded them.

"And whatever else Layer has in store," Anna added.

Leo was already busy organizing his finds. "I've started cataloging plant samples. Some of these may have medicinal properties".

"I'll study any signs or markings we find along the way. Every clue matters," Teitra agreed.

That night, under the unchanging sun, they took turns keeping a vigilant watch. The endless plains whispered continuously around them, feeling intensely alive with ancient secrets and unseen eyes. The rest period passed quietly, broken only by the soft rustling of tall grasses and the distant, haunting calls from unseen creatures.

When they broke camp, the golden light was still casting its long shadows over the endless sea of green. Marche meticulously adjusted the heavy leather breastplate strapped tightly across his chest and thoroughly checked the grip on his cast iron dagger. He breathed deeply, taking in the rich scent of earth and wildflowers.

"East," Marche said decisively, pointing toward the horizon where the sun hung frozen in the sky. "The gate lies beyond these plains. We keep moving".

Anna smoothly slung her boltgun over her shoulder, her fingers brushing against the worn leather of her own breastplate. Her red eyes scanned the horizon, sharp and acutely alert. "Something's changed," she murmured. "The wildlife is quieter... too quiet".

Leo tightened the thick straps of his aluminum fiber vest, his yellow eyes narrowing as he intensely observed the unnatural stillness surrounding them. His slingshot hung readily at his side. "The air feels different. I'll keep watch for anything unusual".

Teitra held her compass steady, her own cast iron dagger gleaming faintly at her hip. "The runes we found spoke of guardians and paths. We're close. Stay vigilant".

Suddenly, a low, terrifying growl shattered the silence. From the tall grass emerged a pack of sleek, shadowy creatures, their eyes glowing with a feral hunger.

"Defensive positions!" Marche commanded instantly, drawing his heavy dagger.

Anna swiftly nocked a bolt, her boltgun aimed and ready. "I've got their flank!".

Leo ducked behind a nearby rock, loading his slingshot with practiced, steady hands. "If they get close, I'll keep them at bay".

Teitra's voice rose in a steady, melodic chant, weaving protective magical wards that shimmered like a veil around the group. The battle was incredibly fierce but ultimately brief. Stones and heavy bolts flew through the air as spells flared brightly, forcing the wounded creatures to eventually retreat back into the grass.

Breathing heavily, Marche looked at his adrenaline-fueled team. "This is only the beginning. Layer is dangerous".

Leo wiped a layer of sweat from his brow. "Their venom is unlike anything I've seen. I need to study it".

Teitra nodded in agreement. "Every encounter teaches us something new".

As the sun continued to shine brilliantly in the sky, the team pressed onward. They soon came upon a half-buried stone marker, its surface inscribed with ancient runes that glowed with a faint, pulsing light. Teitra gently traced the symbols with her fingertips. "This language... it's old, but I can decipher parts. It speaks of 'guardians' and 'paths.' We're on the right track".

Marche smiled, a fierce pride in his chest. "Then we move forward. Together". The Endless Plains stretched before them, vast and mysterious, but their shared bond grew stronger with every single step they took into the unknown.

As they walked, Marche's gaze drifted toward the horizon, the endless grass shimmering beneath the unchanging sun. His heart raced—not merely from excitement, but from the crushing weight of responsibility. His leather breastplate felt heavier with each passing step, serving as a constant, physical reminder of the lethal dangers ahead. His fingers instinctively brushed the hilt of his cast iron dagger, finding a familiar comfort in an entirely unfamiliar world. I have to lead them well. I can't let anyone down, he told himself. He glanced back at his team, a quiet, reassuring smile tugging at his lips. "Stay close. We move as one". His voice was perfectly steady, but inside, his brilliant mind raced with endless plans and contingencies. The thrill of the exploration was undeniably intoxicating, but he knew this was only the beginning of a far greater, deadlier challenge.

Anna's red eyes relentlessly scanned the tall grasses and distant treelines, every muscle in her body coiled tight like a spring. Her boltgun rested lightly against her shoulder, her fingers twitching in absolute readiness. She was deeply captivated by the beauty surrounding her—the vibrant wildflowers, the endless expanse of sky—but her insatiable curiosity was now heavily tempered by caution. There's more here than meets the eye. Every shadow could hide a secret, every whisper a warning, she thought. She paused briefly, crouching down to examine a strange, exotic flower whose petals shimmered faintly. "Look at this," she murmured, her voice filled with pure wonder. "Layer's alive in ways we don't understand yet". Her passion for discovery was fierce, but beneath it lay a profound, unshakeable desire to protect her friends and uncover the ultimate truth.

Leo's green hair fell into his eyes as he knelt to carefully inspect a patch of unique grass. His yellow eyes flickered with intense focus as he cataloged the plant's structure and hypothesized its potential properties. The aluminum fiber vest he wore shifted slightly as he moved; it was expertly designed to offer protection without hindering his meticulous, delicate work. He barely noticed the broader world around him, completely absorbed in the complex science of survival. "This species could have medicinal uses," he muttered, rapidly jotting notes on a small tablet. Yet, even as his brilliant mind raced with scientific hypotheses, a flicker of genuine concern crossed his face. *I need to stay aware,* he realized. *One mistake here could cost us dearly.*

Teitra walked with a quiet, undeniable grace, her fiery red hair catching the eternal sunlight. Her golden eyes held a calm intelligence as she held her brass compass perfectly steady. She listened not just to the overt sounds around her, but to the subtle, vital rhythms of her teammates—the hitch in their breaths, the cadence of their footsteps, and the weight of their unspoken worries. Her extensive training in languages and vocal cues made her highly attuned to nuances that others might completely miss. When Leo spoke softly about a plant's properties, she caught the faint hesitation in his voice. When Anna's eyes darted anxiously toward the horizon, she sensed the unspoken questions lingering in her mind. *We're stronger together,* she thought, a gentle, protective smile touching her lips. *And I'll be their voice when words fail.*

As the sun seemed to climb slightly higher, the group paused by a small, crystalline stream. Marche filled their water skins while Anna kept a sharp, diligent watch. Leo knelt beside the flowing water, dipping his fingers in and murmuring quiet theories about its mineral content. Teitra sat comfortably nearby, quietly translating an ancient phrase they had found etched onto a nearby stone.

Marche broke the peaceful silence. "It's moments like these that remind me why we do this—not just for knowledge, but for each other".

Anna nodded in agreement, slowly lowering her boltgun. "Every step we take, every danger we face, we face together".

Leo looked up from his extensive notes, a rare, genuine softness in his voice. "I'm glad to have you all with me".

Teitra smiled warmly at them all. "And I'll make sure our story is told—every triumph, every challenge". She playfully splashed a handful of water lightly toward the medic. "You know, Leo, if you spent half as much time noticing me as you do those plants, you might actually get my directions right".

Leo, without even looking up from the stream, replied, "Directions? I'm focused on the minerals here. You know how important this is".

"Oh, I know," Teitra grinned. "But maybe some minerals aren't as interesting as the person standing right next to you".

Leo frowned slightly, utterly confused. "Wait, what? I'm standing right here?".

"Exactly. Right here," Teitra teased. "Maybe next time you'll look up from your notes and notice me".

Leo laughed nervously, entirely missing the cue. "I'm pretty sure I notice everything important. Like how this water's pH is perfectly balanced".

Teitra playfully nudged his shoulder. "Sure, Mr. Science. But I'm hoping you'll notice more than just the water someday".

"Well, if you're talking about hydration levels, I'm all ears," Leo remained completely oblivious.

Teitra let out a soft, fond laugh. "One day, Leo. One day".

A few feet away, Anna glanced over at the exchange by the stream, a soft, amused smile tugging at her lips. "You see that? Leo's completely clueless, isn't he?".

Marche chuckled, adjusting the heavy fit of his leather breastplate as he watched Leo intently studying the water while Teitra teased him effortlessly. "Clueless is putting it mildly. It's like he's got tunnel vision when it comes to science".

Anna laughed quietly. "You'd think after all this time, he'd catch on to what Teitra's trying to say".

Marche shook his head with a wide grin. "Maybe he's just too focused on the minerals to notice anything else. Or maybe he's waiting for the right moment... if there ever is one".

Anna nudged him playfully, her tone shifting slightly. "Speaking of moments... what about us?".

Marche's smile faltered for a heartbeat before he looked away, nervously rubbing the back of his neck. "Yeah... maybe. But watching Leo, I'm reminded that some things take time—and courage". They shared a quiet, understanding laugh, the unspoken feelings between them hanging in the air as they continued to watch their friends, both hopeful and incredibly patient.

When they gathered their gear, the morning sun was casting long shadows across the endless sea of grass once more. Marche took a deep breath, steadying his nerves. "The gate lies ahead," he stated, his voice firm but calm. "We keep moving east".

Anna confidently slung her boltgun over her shoulder, her red eyes actively scanning the horizon for any signs of danger. Leo adjusted the tight straps of his aluminum fiber vest, his gaze focused heavily on the terrain while his brilliant mind raced with fresh observations. Teitra held the brass compass perfectly steady, her golden eyes reflecting pure determination. Step by step, they pressed forward, the tall grasses whispering around them as the sun's unchanging light warmed their backs, drawing them deeper into the vast unknown. The endless plains stretched out before them, vast and mysterious, but their powerful bond grew tangibly stronger with every step.

As the team pressed eastward, the peaceful hum of the Endless Plains shattered violently. The tall grass ahead rippled with erratic, violent movement, and a low, terrifyingly guttural growl echoed through the air.

Anna’s grip tightened on her boltgun. "Something's coming. Stay sharp".

From the shadows of the deep grass burst a massive pack of snarling Shadowfangs—sleek, highly lethal wolf-like predators with fur that seemed to literally absorb the surrounding light, their eyes glowing a fierce, terrifying crimson. Their razor-sharp teeth glistened wetly as they lunged viciously toward the team.

Marche drew his cast iron dagger, stepping bravely forward to meet the lethal charge. "Form a circle! Protect the medic!".

Leo swiftly loaded his slingshot, aiming directly for the lead predator. "These creatures' venom is potent. Aim for the head!".

Teitra chanted softly and rapidly, weaving complex magical wards that shimmered like a translucent, protective shield around them, dampening the sheer ferocity of the beasts.

But the danger was far from over. From the nearby, scattered trees, a new nightmare emerged—Thornclaws. These massive reptilian beasts were covered in jagged, terrifying spines and dripped with venomous barbs. They hissed menacingly, their cold eyes locked onto the intruders.

Anna fired bolt after heavy bolt, each shot incredibly precise and deadly. "Watch your flanks! Thornclaws are fast!".

Marche parried a devastating swipe from a Thornclaw's massive claw, countering seamlessly with a swift, brutal strike to its softer side. Leo moved quickly through the chaos, applying a rapid dose of salve to a shallow wound that had opened on Anna's arm. The battle raged fiercely, pushing the team's coordination and resolve to their absolute physical limits. Together, they fought back the deadly creatures, their unbreakable unity finally turning the tide of the skirmish.

As the very last Shadowfang fled into the brush and the wounded Thornclaws retreated, the team stood breathless but unbroken. Marche sheathed his dagger, his eyes scanning the horizon for secondary threats. "This is only the beginning. Layer's dangers are real—and relentless".

Leo nodded, his mind already churning on how to properly study the deadly venom. "We'll need every advantage if we're to survive".

Teitra's voice was remarkably steady as she worked to reinforce their fading wards. "And every lesson learned will bring us closer to the gate".

Anna wiped a layer of sweat from her brow, her red eyes fierce. "Let's keep moving. The plains won't wait".

They gathered in a tight, defensive circle, their breaths heavy and bodies tense from the sudden skirmish. The endless grass swayed gently around them, entirely indifferent to the fierce battle that had just unfolded upon its soil. Leo knelt down first, urgently inspecting Anna's arm where a shallow claw mark bled slowly. His fingers moved deftly, applying a cooling, medicinal salve with practiced care. "The venom in their claws is fast-acting but not fatal if treated quickly. We need to stay vigilant for symptoms".

Anna flexed her fingers, wincing slightly but nodding her appreciation. "Thanks, Leo. Couldn't have held them off without you".

Marche's eyes scanned the horizon thoughtfully. "We underestimated how many predators roam these plains. We need a better plan moving forward".

Teitra stepped forward, her golden eyes sharp as she held her compass perfectly steady. "We should adjust our pace and formation. I suggest a tighter circle when moving through dense grass or near tree lines".

Anna agreed without hesitation, aggressively loading a fresh bolt into her boltgun. "I can cover the rear and flanks. If anything approaches again, I'll signal immediately".

Leo added his own contingency plan. "I'll prepare additional antidotes and keep a close watch on everyone's health. We can't afford to be caught off guard".

Marche nodded, officially rallying the group. "Good. We move cautiously but steadily. Every step brings us closer to the gate—and the answers we seek". They took a vital moment to rest, sharing water and quiet words of encouragement; the fight had severely tested their strength and resolve, but their bond had only grown stronger.

Anna sat on a smooth stone, her fingers gently pressing the edges of the shallow claw mark on her forearm. The faint sting lingered, but she expertly masked it with a determined smile as Marche approached, his bright blue eyes filled with heavy concern.

"Anna," Marche began softly, dropping to kneel beside her, "that wound—are you sure you're alright? You didn't say much back there".

She met his gaze head-on, her red eyes entirely steady. "It's nothing serious, Marche. Leo's salve is working. I'll be fine".

Marche's brow furrowed tightly. "I know you're tough, but you can't push yourself too hard. We need you at your best".

Anna sighed, a rare flicker of vulnerability momentarily crossing her face. "I hate slowing the team down. But... I'll be more careful".

He reached out, placing a firm, reassuring hand on her shoulder. "You're not alone in this. We watch out for each other. Promise me you'll speak up if it gets worse".

A small, genuine smile returned to her lips. "I promise. Thanks, Marche". For a fleeting moment, the vast, terrifying plains around them seemed to fade away completely, leaving only the quiet, profound understanding between two comrades bound by far more than just duty.

Still worried, Marche approached Leo, who was meticulously examining some plant samples near the remnants of their campfire. His green hair fell slightly over his intense yellow eyes, deep in scientific thought as usual.

"Leo," Marche began, intentionally keeping his voice low, "Anna's wound looked worse than she lets on. Can you keep an eye on it? Make sure it doesn't get infected or worsen".

Leo glanced up, his expression calm but extremely serious. "I noticed the claw mark too. The salve should help, but the venom can be insidious. I'll monitor her closely—check for swelling, fever, any signs of toxin spread".

Marche nodded appreciatively, relief washing over him. "She's tough, but I don't want her pushing herself too hard. We need her sharp".

Leo gave a small, almost imperceptible nod of solidarity. "I'll make sure she rests when needed. If anything changes, I'll let you know immediately".

Marche placed a hand briefly on the medic's shoulder. "Thanks. It means a lot".

Leo's gaze softened just a bit. "She's a vital part of this team. I'll do everything I can".

Turning his protective instincts to the rest of his team, Leo later stood near the flickering campfire, his gaze fixed intently on Teitra as she carefully cleaned her cast iron dagger. The warm glow of the flames danced beautifully across her red hair, and for a moment, he hesitated before finally speaking.

"Teitra... during the fight, you moved so fast," Leo started, his voice quieter than usual, tinged with a genuine, uncharacteristic concern. "Are you sure you didn't get hurt? I mean, I didn't see any injuries, but... you never know".

Teitra looked up, genuinely surprised by the softness in his tone. "I'm fine, Leo. Just a few scratches. Nothing serious".

Leo's eyes lingered on her for a moment longer than strictly necessary. "You have to be careful. I... I don't want anything to happen to you". His words slipped out almost unconsciously, and his cheeks immediately flushed a deep shade of green in his embarrassment.

Teitra's lips curved into a wonderfully gentle smile. "Thank you, Leo. That means a lot". She paused, then couldn't resist teasing lightly, "You're not usually this... worried".

Leo cleared his throat incredibly awkwardly. "I-I'm just doing my job as the medic. Someone has to keep everyone alive".

Teitra laughed softly. "Well, I'm glad it's you".

Leo looked away quickly, scratching the back of his neck to hide his flush. "Yeah... me too".

As the sun continued to shine fixedly in the sky, the team rose together once more, entirely ready to face whatever new challenges the Endless Plains—and Layer itself—would throw at them. Morning light—or what passed for it—filtered softly through the endless sky, casting a warm glow over the rolling grasses. Yet, as always, the sun hung motionless at its zenith, unmoving and eternal, acting as a silent sentinel over the strange world beneath the earth.

The team stirred from their camp, stretching weary limbs and preparing for another grueling day's journey. Marche tightened the straps of his leather breastplate and checked the razor edge of his cast iron dagger, his blue eyes scanning the horizon with steady, absolute resolve. Anna gathered her gear, slinging her boltgun securely over her shoulder, her red eyes bright with raw determination despite the lingering ache in her arm. Leo carefully packed his fragile medical supplies, adjusting the aluminum fiber vest that protected him, his gaze thoughtful as he reviewed his meticulous notes on the recent encounter. Teitra held the compass firmly in her grip, her golden eyes reflecting the unwavering needle as she led the way forward. Without speaking a word, they moved as one, the tall grasses whispering softly around their boots. Step by step, they pressed eastward, venturing deeper into the mysteries of Layer, bound by an unbreakable purpose and trust.

The tall grasses of the Endless Plains suddenly stilled, and an eerie silence violently fell over the land—an unspoken but deeply felt warning.

From the dense shadows emerged a horrifying swarm of strange creatures: sleek, terrifying insectoid beasts. Their chitinous armor shimmered unnaturally under the eternal sun, their many legs clicking ominously in the silence as they advanced en masse. Their eyes glowed with a cold, entirely alien intelligence.

Anna raised her boltgun swiftly, firing incredibly precise bolts that managed to pierce the creatures' tough exoskeletons. "They're everywhere! Watch your flanks!" she shouted, her voice sharp with rising urgency.

Marche drew his cast iron dagger, aggressively stepping protectively in front of Anna. "Stay close! Don't let them surround us!".

Leo scrambled to prepare his slingshot, frantically loading it with carefully crafted pellets specifically designed to pierce heavy armor. "These creatures' carapaces are tough, but not impenetrable. Aim for the joints!".

Teitra's voice rose in a desperate, steady chant, weaving protective magical wards that shimmered around the team to dampen the creatures' relentless attacks.

The battle was fiercely chaotic. Despite their excellent coordination, a creature broke through Anna's defenses, slashing her arm brutally with venomous claws. She staggered back, a sharp cry escaping her lips as dark blood seeped visibly through her leather breastplate.

Marche's blue eyes blazed with an uncontainable fury. "Anna!" he roared, his voice echoing fiercely across the plains. With a truly feral growl, he charged recklessly into the swarm, his dagger flashing as he cut down the attackers with a terrifying, renewed vigor.

Leo rushed to Anna's side instantly, quickly applying a potent salve to her deep wound. "Hold still, Anna. The venom's potent, but I'll slow its spread".

Anna gritted her teeth in agony, nodding despite the overwhelming pain. "Thanks, Leo... and thanks, Marche. I'm okay".

Marche's gaze hardened into steel as he scanned the bloodied battlefield. "No creature in Layer will hurt my team without paying the price". With fierce determination, the team rallied together, aggressively pushing back the swarm until the very last creature fled back into the tall grass. Breathing heavily, they regrouped, their bond hardened by the brutal trial.

Marche knelt beside Anna, his voice much softer now. "You're not just my teammate. You're family. We keep moving, but we watch out for each other".

Anna managed a tired, pain-filled smile. "Always".

As the adrenaline of the battle slowly faded, Anna's steps grew visibly uneven, her breath becoming shallow and labored. The deep wound on her arm throbbed fiercely, and a cold, sickly sweat broke across her pale forehead.

"Anna?" Marche's voice was sharp with extreme concern as he caught her just as she stumbled, steadying her with firm, protective hands.

"I... I don't feel well," she whispered weakly, her normally vivid red eyes dimming heavily with fatigue. "I can't keep going".

Without a second of hesitation, Marche lifted her gently into his arms, the physical weight heavier than he expected but no less precious to him. "I've got you," he said quietly. "We'll find a safe place to rest".

Leo hurried anxiously beside them, his eyes frantically scanning Anna for signs of worsening venom effects. "Her vitals are dropping. We need to move quickly but carefully".

Teitra supported Marche's steady pace, her voice providing a soothing murmur as she actively reinforced the protective wards around their retreating group. "We're almost there. Just a little further".

The team pressed urgently on through the swaying grass until they finally reached a sheltered clearing, shielded completely by ancient trees and bathed in soft, dappled light. Carefully, reverently, Marche laid Anna down on a soft bed of moss and ferns. Leo immediately set to work, preparing significantly stronger antidotes and expertly tending to her wound with practiced hands. Teitra knelt loyally by Anna's side, whispering calming words and continuously maintaining the magical wards. Marche sat extremely close, his hand never once leaving hers. "Rest now, Anna. We'll keep watch. You're not alone".

Anna's eyes fluttered closed, a faint, grateful smile touching her lips despite the excruciating pain. "Thank you, Marche... for everything". As the sun hung perfectly still in the sky, the team settled into a deeply vigilant quiet, bound firmly by hope and the unspoken strength of their shared journey.

The dappled light of the clearing filtered softly through the leaves as Anna lay resting on the moss. Leo carefully finished applying his remedies, his hands remarkably steady despite the grave urgency of the moment. The venom's intense sting had finally dulled, and the fever that had tightly gripped her began to ebb away. Marche sat intimately close by, his strong hand gently holding Anna's pale one. His blue eyes softened significantly as he watched her chest rise and fall with slow, even breaths. Fatigue tugged heavily at him, and before long, his eyelids grew irresistibly heavy. Settling down beside her, he allowed himself a brief, well-earned moment of rest, his fingers never leaving hers.

Nearby, Teitra and Leo stood quietly, their voices hushed as they deeply discussed the dire situation.

"She looks peaceful now, but that venom was unlike anything we've seen. Are you sure she'll recover fully?" Teitra asked.

Leo nodded confidently. "The treatment should buy her time. The venom and fever will subside with rest. She's strong—her body just needs to heal".

Teitra looked at him with profound gratitude. "We're lucky to have you with us. Without your knowledge, this could have been much worse".

Leo shrugged modestly. "I just do what I can. But we all have to be vigilant. Layer isn't forgiving".

Teitra glanced back at Marche and Anna sleeping peacefully. "We'll keep watch. They need us to be ready".

Leo's gaze followed hers. "Agreed. For now, rest is the best medicine". As the two stood guard, the clearing was filled with a quiet, profound calm, the team's bond deepening immensely in the shared silence. Somewhere beyond the trees, the vast mysteries of Layer awaited, but here, for a brief moment, there was only healing and hope.

Anna's eyes fluttered open to the soft glow of the unchanging sun filtering through the canopy. Her gaze settled warmly on Marche's face, peaceful and watchful beside her. Her fingers instinctively found his, and she smiled softly, feeling the deep warmth of his hand still wrapped securely around hers. The terrifying fever that had gripped her earlier was completely gone, beautifully replaced by a refreshing clarity and a physical strength she hadn't expected to regain so quickly.

Gently, she nudged Marche's shoulder. "Marche... wake up," she whispered.

Marche stirred immediately, his blue eyes opening slowly, clouded heavily with concern before they brightened significantly at the sight of her awake. "Anna? How do you feel?".

"Almost one hundred percent," she replied brightly, sitting up carefully. "Thanks to Leo".

Marche helped her to her feet, steadying her firmly with a supportive arm. "Good. Let's pack up. We can't stay here forever".

As they gathered their scattered belongings, Marche turned to Leo, who was already deeply engrossed in checking his notes. "Thanks for everything, Leo. You saved her".

Leo nodded quietly. "It was a team effort. And thanks to Teitra for keeping watch".

Teitra smiled radiantly, brushing a stray lock of fiery red hair behind her ear. "We make a good team".

Marche looked back at Anna, offering his arm chivalrously. "Let me carry you for a while longer. You need to conserve your strength".

Anna's cheeks flushed a bright red, and she pulled away slightly in her embarrassment. "No way. I'm walking on my own... for now".

Teitra laughed softly at the display. "Well, Leo, if you want to carry me, I sure wouldn't mind".

Leo glanced up, a faint, oblivious smile tugging at his lips. "Thanks, but carrying people would get in the way of my research".

Teitra rolled her eyes playfully. "Maybe next time then".

The team shared a lighthearted moment before setting off once more, their bonds irrevocably strengthened by the trials faced and overcome, entirely ready to face whatever mysteries Layer held next.

After hours of steady walking through the endless sway of the grass, the team's pace dramatically slowed as a remarkable, impossible sight emerged on the horizon. Rising solemnly from the exact center of a vast clearing stood a massive stone doorway, deeply weathered by time yet incredibly imposing and resolute. It stood completely alone, an ancient sentinel anchored in the sea of green, its sheer surface carved with intricate runes that pulsed faintly with a soft, otherworldly glow.

Marche was the first to stop, his breath physically catching as he took in the sheer grandeur of the gate. "There it is," he said quietly, his eyes fixed on the towering arch. "The gate the legends spoke of".

Anna lowered her boltgun, stepping forward with cautious awe. "It's... unlike anything I imagined. So much history etched into every stone".

Leo knelt beside a patch of grass near the clearing’s edge, carefully examining the soil and the faint, palpable magical residue lingering heavily in the air. "The energy here is strong. Whatever lies beyond, it's protected—and powerful".

Teitra approached the gate, her fingers gently tracing the glowing runes. "These inscriptions... they speak of trials and guardians. We'll need all our strength and wits to pass through".

Marche turned to his team, absolute determination shining brightly in his blue eyes. "We've come this far together. Whatever awaits us beyond this doorway, we face it as one".

The team stood united before the towering stone gate, its ancient runes glowing faintly in the soft light of the clearing. Teitra stepped forward, her golden eyes narrowing as she focused intensely on the intricate symbols carved deep into the stone. Slowly, magical words began to shimmer and hover in the air before her—ethereal, glowing letters only she could see, floating like whispers in a forgotten language. Her voice was incredibly soft but perfectly clear as she began to read the runes aloud, carefully following the sequence as the words danced in front of her.

The gate responded, rumbling deeply with ancient power. Slowly, the massive stone doors began to part, revealing a blinding light that spilled outward into the clearing. Marche shielded his eyes as the brilliant glow finally faded, unveiling a dense, deeply twisted forest located inexplicably beyond the threshold. The canopy was incredibly thick and dark, the branches curling into unnatural shapes that seemed to reach out like grasping fingers. The air was noticeably cooler here, heavy with the scent of damp earth and profound mystery. Marche glanced back at the gate's exterior, which now appeared as if it had never moved—a solid, perfectly closed door. The magic of Layer was subtle and dangerously deceptive.

Before stepping forward into the dark, Anna brushed past Marche, her cheeks flushed with adrenaline. She pressed a quick, warm kiss to his cheek, her red eyes sparkling with a potent mixture of excitement and nerves. Without hesitation, she leapt boldly through the gate and disappeared entirely into the shadowed forest.

Teitra followed swiftly, reaching Leo and planting a gentle, affectionate kiss on his cheek. Her eyes met his with a teasing smile before she too vanished gracefully into the dark woods.

Marche and Leo exchanged a long glance—both slightly embarrassed but smiling genuinely. The unspoken feelings lingered heavily between them for a moment before Marche took a steadying breath and stepped confidently through the gate, Leo following close behind. Together, they entered the twisted forest, the heavy shadows closing around them as their next great adventure began.

Chapter 2
A Twisted Forest

The moment they stepped through the shimmering threshold of the gate, the air grew incredibly thick, suffocating them with a strange, heavy energy. The brilliant, eternal sunlight of the Endless Plains was instantly swallowed by the dense, impenetrable canopy of the Twisted Forest. Above them, gnarled branches curled and tangled like the arthritic claws of ancient giants, choking out the sky. Shadows danced erratically across the damp earth, and the rich, pungent scent of wet moss and decaying wood filled their lungs.

Marche caught up to Anna just as she paused to take in the shadowed expanse, her red eyes wide with a mixture of profound wonder and stubborn defiance.

"Anna," Marche said, his voice dropping to a low, earnest register that cut through the eerie quiet of the woods. "I love your adventurous spirit. I truly do. But you shouldn't have leaped through the gate blindly like that. We have no idea what's waiting on the other side."

Anna's cheeks flushed a deep, vivid crimson. Her usual unwavering confidence faltered entirely under the weight of his intense gaze and his unexpected choice of words. "You... you actually said you love my spirit?" she stammered, entirely caught off guard by the raw sincerity in his tone.

Before Marche could respond and navigate the sudden, heavy tension between them, Teitra materialized beside them, her face alight with a joyous, teasing energy. She was so caught up in the romantic tension radiating from her friends that she stepped backward, accidentally bumping hard into Leo, who was already deeply engrossed in walking and writing in his journal simultaneously.

"Oh! Sorry, Leo!" Teitra gasped. She grabbed his arms to steady herself, her grip lingering just a fraction too long and a bit too tight.

Leo's notes fluttered from his hands, scattering across the damp forest floor like fallen leaves. He looked down at the mess, then back up at Teitra, a remarkably soft smile spreading across his normally stoic face. "It's alright," he said gently, dropping to one knee to gather the scattered pages.

Teitra immediately knelt beside him to help, her slender fingers intentionally brushing against his as they reached for the same piece of parchment. "You're always so intensely focused," she teased lightly, her golden eyes sparkling in the dim light. "Maybe you need someone to remind you to look up once in a while."

Leo chuckled softly, a warm, resonant sound, and met her gaze directly. "Maybe I do."

Marche and Anna exchanged a knowing glance, the lingering tension from their own exchange easing into a comfortable, shared warmth. In a world entirely defined by the unknown, the team was finding an unshakable strength in their bonds.

But Layer rarely allowed for extended moments of peace.

As the team took a few cautious steps away from the glowing gate, a deafening, earth-shaking *thud* echoed behind them. The team whipped around just in time to see the massive stone doors slam violently shut. The intricate runes that had bathed the clearing in their ethereal light flickered once, desperately, and then died. The gate was now as silent and lifeless as a tombstone.

Anna's breath caught in her throat. "It's closed… and the runes are dead. We're trapped."

Marche reached out, his calloused fingers gently finding hers and intertwining them. His blue eyes met her panicked red ones with absolute, unyielding reassurance. "For now, just walk with me. We will find a way through this—together."

Anna hesitated, the thrill of the adventure suddenly overshadowed by the claustrophobic reality of their confinement. But feeling the steady warmth of his hand, she nodded. "Okay… together."

As they moved deeper into the forest, a heavy, oppressive stillness settled around them. Teitra and Leo flanked the pair, their weapons drawn and senses fully alert. Yet, despite their hyper-vigilance, a deeply unsettling presence lingered just beyond their line of sight—a silent watcher hidden securely in the pitch-black shadows. The forest felt alive, its twisted forms whispering threats and forgotten secrets.

"Stay close," Marche ordered, his grip tightening on Anna's hand. "This forest doesn't forgive mistakes."

As they cautiously advanced through the thick undergrowth, a subtle, unnatural movement caught Anna's keen eyes. A few paces ahead, partially obscured by a tangle of thick vines and rotted roots, stood a creature unlike anything they could have ever imagined.

It was roughly the size of a human adult. Its body was heavily armored with a hard, glossy, iridescent shell that covered its chest and arms, reminiscent of a massive beetle's exoskeleton. Yet, extending down its back and cresting its head was a striking mohawk of vibrant feathers that ruffled softly with the damp breeze. Most unsettling of all were its facial features—a sharp, avian beak framed by eyes that were undeniably human. They held an uncanny, terrifying intelligence.

The creature moved with deliberate caution, leaving behind a slick, glistening trail of slimy sludge on the forest floor. Its human eyes flicked toward the team, studying them with a complex mixture of wariness and deep intrigue.

Leo's scientific mind raced. He knelt into the dirt to observe the creature from a safe distance, completely mesmerized. "Fascinating," he murmured, pulling out a fresh notebook. "Its anatomy is a bizarre fusion of insectoid and avian traits, perfectly combined with surprisingly human-like features. I'll call it an 'Insectanaught'."

Marche exchanged a deeply wary glance with Anna. "Why would it have human features, Leo? Is it some kind of rapid evolution, or... something else entirely?"

Teitra stepped forward cautiously, her Orator's training analyzing the creature's subtle vocalizations and rigid body language. "Its communication patterns are highly complex. It might be far more intelligent than we expect. Or perhaps... it's part of Layer's deeper, darker mysteries."

"That creature didn't look natural," Anna whispered, shivering as the Insectanaught blinked slowly and dissolved silently back into the shadows. "Like it was constructed. Made, not born."

Leo adjusted his notes, his brow furrowed in grim realization. "From a scientific perspective, it completely defies normal evolutionary patterns. The fusion suggests artificial manipulation. Bioengineering."

Teitra's golden eyes widened with concern. "If that's true, then Layer isn't just a subterranean ecosystem. Someone—or something—has been actively altering life down here. Creating guardians. Or experiments."

"To keep intruders out," Marche finished, his jaw tightening. "We aren't just exploring anymore. We're trespassing in a laboratory shaped by unknown hands."

The profound weight of this discovery settled heavily over the team. If Layer was engineered, every step forward was a step into an ancient, calculated trap.

Walking a few paces ahead to scout the trail, Marche spoke in a hushed tone to Leo. "If no one has ever returned from beyond the

Endless Plains, how did Paldyne and Melmori manage it all those years ago? If the gates seal behind you... how did they get back up the well?"

"It's a mystery," Leo admitted, his yellow eyes scanning the dense canopy. "The fact that they survived means a return path exists. It just might require knowledge or power we don't possess yet."

"Which means we keep our eyes open for clues," Marche said firmly. "Anything that might show us what the first Hero left behind."

Behind them, Anna leaned closer to Teitra, whispering with a mischievous glint in her eye. "You know, if Leo ever took the leap, you two would make a pretty cute couple."

Marche, overhearing, chuckled quietly, a faint blush coloring his cheeks. "This place does seem to bring out what's been hidden. For all of us." Anna smiled, wrapping her arm securely around Marche's as their steps fell into a perfect, unified rhythm.

Eventually, the claustrophobic density of the forest gave way to a breathtaking, terrifying expanse. The trees cleared at the edge of a massive, sheer ravine carved deep into the earth. From high above, a powerful, roaring waterfall thundered over the precipice, sending a permanent cloud of mist swirling into the air as it crashed into a violent river far below.

Spanning the terrifying drop was a long, narrow wooden rope bridge. It swayed precariously in the wind, its weathered planks and frayed ropes serving as a grim testament to decades of rot and exposure.

Anna peered across the gap, her red eyes catching sight of a structure on the far cliffs. "There," she pointed.

Nestled on the opposite side was a small log cabin. It was almost entirely swallowed by nature, its wooden walls cloaked in thick vines and heavy moss, blending seamlessly into the dark forest backdrop.

"Fresh water nearby, and signs of deliberate habitation," Leo noted, studying the soil at the edge of the cliff. "That cabin could be a refuge. Or a clue."

"We cross together," Marche ordered. "Stay close and watch your footing."

They stepped onto the swaying bridge, the weathered planks creaking agonizingly beneath their boots. The deafening roar of the waterfall filled their ears, vibrating through their very bones. Marche and Anna moved with practiced balance, stepping off the far end of the bridge and allowing their boots to meet solid earth with a reassuring crunch.

Just as they turned back to guide the others, a sharp, terrified scream pierced the roar of the water.

"Teitra!" Marche shouted.

Near the end of the bridge, a rotted plank had completely given way. Teitra had plunged through the gap, her body dropping wildly toward the abyss.

Moving with pure, unthinking instinct, Leo lunged forward, throwing his body onto the wooden planks. His hand shot through the gap, his fingers locking onto Teitra's wrist in a desperate, iron-clad grip just as she began to fall.

"Hold on! I've got you!" Leo grunted, the muscles in his arm straining against her dead weight.

Teitra dangled over the violent river, her breathing quick and panicked as her free hand scrambled to find purchase on the splintered wood. "I... I'm trying!"

"I won't let go," Leo promised, his voice an anchor of absolute calm amidst the chaos. "Take your time. I'm right here."

With Marche and Anna rushing to grab her other arm, they hauled a trembling Teitra up onto the solid cliffside. She collapsed onto the moss, her chest heaving. Leo knelt beside her, his own breath ragged, and gently steadied her shaking shoulders.

"Quick reflexes, Leo," Marche praised, clapping the medic firmly on the shoulder. "You saved her."

Once Teitra had recovered, the team approached the overgrown log cabin. Anna readied her boltgun, the leather of her breastplate creaking softly as she took a defensive stance behind Marche. Drawing his cast iron dagger, Marche crouched and began meticulously slicing away the thick vines that held the heavy wooden door shut.

The moment his hand touched the iron handle, a loud, frantic scurry echoed from within the dark cabin. The team froze.

Marche and Leo exchanged a knowing glance. Without hesitation, Marche yanked the door open with a forceful, violent motion.

Out leapt a creature straight from a fever dream. It possessed the sleek, agile body of a cat covered in dark fur, but its legs were thin, hairless, and rat-like, ending in razor-sharp claws. A long, hairless tail whipped behind it. But as it turned its head, the team recoiled in horror—its face was entirely human. It possessed wide, expressive eyes and a mouth that opened to release a deep, guttural, and deeply unsettling *meow*.

The chimera struck like lightning, launching itself directly at Marche's chest and knocking the explorer flat onto his back. Before anyone could fire a shot, the creature meowed once more—a sound too intelligent, too mocking—and bounded off the porch, disappearing into the dense foliage.

Marche pushed himself up, shaking his head in disbelief. "What the hell was that?"

"Layer keeps its secrets well," Teitra whispered, sheathing her dagger.

Cautiously, they stepped inside the cabin. The floorboards groaned beneath their weight. Shafts of dim light pierced through cracks in the timber walls, illuminating a thick layer of undisturbed dust. It was a single, sparsely furnished room. A rough-hewn table held a rusted metal cup, an old knife, and a bundle of dried herbs tied with frayed twine.

"The fire in the hearth has been out for decades," Leo observed, kneeling by the ashes. "But these herbs... someone used this place to treat wounds. To survive."

Teitra moved to the far corner, her fingers gently tracing a series of faded symbols etched deep into the wood. "These runes... they're identical to the ones on the gate. Whoever lived here understood the magic of this place. They were hiding from it."

As they prepared to step back outside to scout the perimeter, Teitra's keen eyes caught a subtle, suppressed wince from Leo, followed by an unmistakable limp as he walked. He had pulled a muscle in his leg when he threw himself onto the bridge to save her, and he was trying to hide it so as not to slow the team down.

A fierce wave of protective affection washed over Teitra. She quickly stepped in front of Marche and Anna, raising her hand.

"Wait," Teitra lied smoothly, feigning a wince of her own. "I think my leg might be injured from the fall on the bridge. I can't push on right now. We should rest here for the night."

Marche frowned, his blue eyes narrowing with immediate concern for her. "If that's the case, we stop. This cabin is the best shelter we'll find anyway."

As Marche and Anna turned to build a fire in the hearth, Leo stepped close to Teitra, his cheeks flushing a faint green. He reached out, gently taking her hand. "Thank you for covering for me," he whispered. "I overused my leg pulling you up. But I don't regret it for a second."

Teitra squeezed his hand, her golden eyes warm. "We're a team, Leo. We look out for each other."

As the evening deepened, the warmth of the hearth pushed the chill of the Twisted Forest at bay. Marche and Anna sat huddled in a quiet corner, their hands naturally finding each other in the dark, finding profound comfort in their shared presence. Across the room, Leo curled up on the floorboards. Teitra quietly moved beside him.

"Would you mind if I sat next to you?" she asked softly. "It'll help keep us warm."

"I'd like that," Leo replied gratefully. They sat close, the terrifying weight of Layer momentarily forgotten in the fragile comfort of their proximity.

As the fire's glow dimmed into dying embers, Anna slipped into a deep, heavy sleep.

Her mind was instantly pulled into a vivid, ethereal dream. She was standing outside the very cabin they now slept in, but it wasn't overgrown or dusty. It was bathed in a soft, brilliant white light. Standing on the porch were two figures—a towering, broad-shouldered man with a crimson cape, and a breathtaking woman with hair as pale as moonlight. Paldyne and Melmori.

They spoke in hushed tones, their words a beautiful, foreign melody that Anna couldn't comprehend. But the intimacy between them—the way their hands almost touched, the fierce, protective love in Paldyne's dark eyes—resonated deeply within Anna's soul. It mirrored exactly how she felt about Marche.

Before the dream faded into the dark, Anna watched Paldyne reach toward the cabin door frame. He carefully slipped a small, folded piece of parchment into a hidden crack in the wood.

Anna awoke with a sharp gasp. The cabin was quiet, illuminated only by the morning light filtering through the cracks. The others were already awake. Marche sat nearby, a gentle smile on his face. "You looked too peaceful to wake," he whispered.

"Marche..." Anna breathed, scrambling to her feet, her heart pounding. "There was a note in my dream. Paldyne left it in a crack near the door."

Without waiting for a response, she hobbled over to the doorway, her fingers desperately searching the rotted wood. She found the crack. Her breath hitched as she pulled a fragile, yellowed piece of folded parchment from the timber.

The team gathered around her in absolute awe. "A message from the past," Teitra whispered reverently.

The ink was heavily faded, but the message from the first Hero was clear. Paldyne wrote that the glowing runes etched into the cabin wall were identical to the gate mechanics. He confirmed that the forest was a sanctuary of sorts, populated only by bizarre, relatively harmless chimeras—engineered blends of animals. He warned that speaking the runes was the only way to reveal the true path forward.

Teitra stepped immediately to the etched wall. Her golden eyes narrowed in focus. Exactly as before, ethereal, shimmering words materialized in the air, visible only to her. With absolute clarity, she recited the ancient syllables.

The moment the final word left her lips, a thunderous, earth-shattering crash echoed from outside.

The team burst through the cabin door, weapons drawn. Standing perfectly in the center of the clearing was a massive new gate, its doors thrown wide open like a portal to another world.

But beyond this gateway lay no forest. Instead, it opened to a vast, sun-drenched savannah. Dominating the new landscape was a singular, colossal mountain, its peak completely lost in swirling, dark storm clouds far above. A winding dirt path snaked upward along the steep, rocky slopes.

"This is it," Marche said, his voice ringing with awe and fierce resolve. "Layer 3."

Just as they prepared to step forward, a familiar *meow* echoed from the brush. The human-faced cat chimera darted from the shadows. With a graceful, bounding leap, it sprang straight through the glowing portal, disappearing into the savannah.

"Do we explore this forest more, or do we follow it?" Marche asked, looking at the team.

"The forest is a dead end," Anna decided, gripping her boltgun tight. "The mountain holds the answers."

As they approached the shimmering threshold, Anna’s heart quickened. Without overthinking it, she rushed to Marche, pressing a quick, affectionate kiss to his cheek. She turned to leap blindly through the portal, exactly as she had done on the plains.

But this time, Marche reached out, his strong hand catching her wrist and pulling her gently back. His bright blue eyes met hers with quiet, absolute resolve.

"This time," Marche said softly, intertwining his fingers with hers, "we go through together."

Anna’s smile rivaled the glowing gate. She nodded, squeezing his hand. Side by side, the Explorer and his partner stepped through the threshold.

Behind them, Leo grinned, holding his hand out to Teitra. Her golden eyes sparkled as she took it firmly. Together, they followed their friends, leaving the shadows of the Twisted Forest behind to face whatever nightmares waited on the cursed peaks above the clouds.

CHAPTER 3
Cursed Mountain Peaks Above the Clouds

The team began their grueling ascent along the winding mountain trail. The path quickly narrowed, hugging the steep, treacherous slopes as it spiraled upward toward the storm-choked peak. After the suffocating, damp darkness of the Twisted Forest, the crisp, thin mountain air was a shock to their lungs, carrying the sharp, clean scent of pine needles and resilient wildflowers.

As they climbed higher into the sunlit savannah enveloping the mountain's base, subtle movement stirred in the tall grasses.

"Look there," Anna whispered, her hand instinctively catching Marche's arm. She pointed toward a cluster of vibrant shapes moving gracefully across the plateau below.

Marche squinted against the bright light. Wandering peacefully through the wilds were creatures completely devoid of the horrifying, aggressive traits they had seen in the forest. One such being resembled a living, breathing bouquet. Bright, colorful flowers clustered tightly around a slender humanoid form. Two gentle eyes peeked curiously from the center of the floral mass, its green skin draped elegantly in a delicate vine dress adorned with blooming petals. It moved on two long, slender legs, swaying beautifully with the mountain breeze.

Leo dropped to one knee, pulling a small magnifying lens from his kit to observe the creature from afar. "Fascinating," he whispered, his pencil flying across his journal. "A perfect symbiotic fusion of flora and fauna. I'll call them 'Hortensis.' They seem entirely peaceful. Almost like walking gardens."

But Layer's beauty was always juxtaposed with its brutal edge.

As they continued along the rocky path, another chimera caught their attention. It was humanoid in shape, but its body was entirely encased in rough, jagged, stone-like armor. It possessed no head; instead, a single, massive yellow eyeball sat deeply embedded in the center of its chest, resting just above a wide, gaping, toothless mouth. Its arms ended in massive, heavy crab-like pincers, which it used to relentlessly dig and crush the rocky ground, consuming the stone itself.

Anna shivered, unconsciously stepping closer to Marche. "That one looks… unsettling. Like some kind of living quarry."

"These chimeras are strange hybrids," Marche noted, his hand resting on his dagger. "Part nature, part something else. So far, it hasn't shown hostility, but we can't be complacent."

"Layer's creations are as mysterious as the world itself," Teitra added thoughtfully. "Each step we take reveals more of its secrets."

As they edged past the grinding beast, Marche's innate curiosity—the very trait that made him an Explorer—momentarily eclipsed his caution. Drawing his cast iron dagger, he stepped off the path and moved closer, intent on studying the creature's stone plating firsthand to see if it held any structural weaknesses.

"Marche, don't—" Anna started to warn.

It was too late. As Marche crossed the invisible threshold into its territory, the chimera's massive yellow eye snapped violently toward him. A sudden, grinding roar shattered the quiet mountain air.

Moving with a lightning-fast agility that defied its heavy stone armor, the chimera swung its massive crab-like pincer in a devastating backhand. The blow struck Marche squarely in the chest.

The sheer, concussive force lifted him off his feet, sending him flying backward through the air. He crashed onto the unforgiving rocky ground with a sickening, heavy thud. He didn't even cry out. His body simply went completely limp, his dagger clattering uselessly against the stones.

"Marche!" Anna's scream tore from her throat, raw and utterly terrified.

She rushed to his side, dropping to her knees, her heart hammering a frantic, agonizing rhythm against her ribs. The mountain seemed to hold its breath as the chimera pivoted, its enormous yellow eye fixing maliciously on the fallen explorer, its heavy pincers raising to deliver a fatal, crushing blow.

"The eye!" Teitra yelled urgently. "Aim for the eye! It's the only vulnerable spot!"

Without a second of hesitation, Anna whipped her boltgun up. Tears blurred her vision, but her hands were fueled by pure, unadulterated desperation. She unleashed a rapid, relentless flurry of bolts directly into the creature's glaring yellow eye.

The heavy bolts pierced the soft tissue perfectly. The chimera staggered backward, a violent shudder running through its stone form. With a final, earth-shaking groan, the light in its eye extinguished, and the beast collapsed, crumbling instantly into a lifeless pile of rocks that tumbled harmlessly away down the slope.

Leo was already kneeling beside Marche, his hands quickly moving over his friend's chest and neck. "He's breathing," Leo confirmed, his voice tight. "But he's unconscious. He took a massive hit to the ribs. We need to keep him stable."

Anna grabbed Marche's hand, pressing it to her cheek, a tear finally escaping to track through the dust on her skin. "Stay with us. Please, Marche."

Slowly, agonizingly, Marche's blue eyes fluttered open. The profound confusion in his gaze quickly melted into overwhelming relief as he saw Anna's face hovering over his. He let out a ragged, painful cough, clutching his chest.

"I'm naming that creature a 'Guardian,'" Leo muttered, sitting back with a relieved sigh. "Simple, but fitting."

Anna helped Marche sit up, her grip incredibly steady and fiercely protective. "Let's be more careful. This mountain is full of surprises," she said, her voice shaking.

Marche managed a weak, apologetic smile as he got to his feet, leaning heavily on her shoulder.

Once Leo and Teitra stepped a few paces away to examine the rubble, giving them a moment of privacy, Anna turned to Marche. Her red eyes were glistening with unshed tears, the terrifying reality of how close she had just come to losing him completely shattering her usual composed exterior.

"Marche," she began, her voice trembling violently. "You scared me back there. I thought... I thought I was going to lose you."

Marche looked down at her, his blue eyes filled with a profound, aching regret. He reached up, gently wiping a tear from her cheek with his thumb. "I'm so sorry, Anna. My curiosity... it got the better of me. I should have been more careful."

Anna shook her head firmly, her hands coming up to grip the heavy leather of his breastplate. "You have to promise me. No more reckless moves. You are the Explorer, you lead us, but you cannot throw your life away. Promise me you'll think before you act."

He looked into her vivid red eyes, seeing the depth of her fear and the undeniable, fierce love hiding just beneath it. He reached out, taking her hands gently in his, his thumbs tracing her knuckles.

"I promise," Marche swore, his voice a low, absolute vow. "No more reckless moves. I will be more careful. For you."

The air between them grew incredibly heavy, charged with all the words they had been too afraid to say since stepping onto the Endless Plains. Anna looked up at him, her breath catching. Without hesitation, she closed the distance, rising on her toes to press her lips to his.

It was a soft, tender kiss—a beautiful, desperate collision of relief, profound affection, and something far deeper. It was their first truly intimate moment, a fragile, unbreakable bridge constructed between friendship and an enduring, protective love. Marche's hands moved to her waist, pulling her flush against him, completely ignoring the burning pain in his ribs.

When they finally pulled back, Marche's cheeks were flushed a deep red, matching Anna's own beautiful blush. They stared into each other's eyes, a quiet, profound reassurance passing between them.

"Let's keep moving..." Anna whispered softly, a small, genuine smile breaking through. "...if you're still up to it today."

Marche nodded, his heart infinitely lighter despite his bruised body. "I'm with you. Always."

The winding mountain path stretched steeply upward, the air growing noticeably thinner and much cooler with every passing hour. The team moved with hyper-vigilance now, their senses painfully alert to the strange life thriving in the alien realm above the clouds.

As they rounded a jagged bend, shadows began to flicker rapidly against the pale sky.

Teitra was the first to spot them. "Look up," she warned, her voice tight with tension.

Hovering overhead was a swarm of massive, horrifying creatures. They were giant, mosquito-like chimeras. Their bodies were slick and segmented, adorned with multiple sets of rapid-beating, bird-like wings that created a deafening, high-pitched hum. Long, repulsive tails made of dripping, acidic slime trailed behind them, while sharp, multi-jointed clawed legs dangled menacingly beneath their monstrous forms.

"They're gathering," Anna noted, her eyes narrowing as she raised her boltgun. "Preparing to dive."

Marche, ignoring the agonizing flare in his chest, shifted into a defensive stance, his dagger at the ready. "Stay close. Don't let them separate us."

The creatures suddenly folded their wings and plunged from the sky, diving with terrifying, predatory speed.

The team scattered. Anna moved swiftly, intentionally positioning herself between the diving swarm and Marche's injured side. Her boltgun barked, firing precise, lethal bolts that tore through the thin mountain air. She struck one chimera in the wing, sending it spiraling out of control into the rocky abyss below.

Another chimera lunged directly at Marche, its claws slashing viciously. He parried with his dagger, gritting his teeth against the pain radiating through his ribs, driving the beast back. Leo crouched low behind a boulder, slinging sharp stones with incredible velocity, aiming directly for the creatures' multifaceted eyes and delicate wing joints. Beside him, Teitra chanted rapidly, weaving protective magical wards that shimmered like a translucent dome around them, dampening the sheer kinetic force of the creatures' strikes.

The battle raged fiercely. Wings beat frantically, kicking up blinding dust, while razor-sharp claws snapped mere inches from exposed flesh. Anna moved with a fierce, uncompromising determination, every single shot perfectly calculated to keep Marche safe. Finally, with a well-placed bolt, she struck the largest chimera directly in its eye. It shrieked, crashing heavily onto the rocky slope and sliding off the cliff edge.

Breathing heavily, the team regrouped as the surviving mosquitoes fled into the clouds. Marche's gaze met Anna's, profound gratitude and deep admiration shining in his eyes.

"We make a good team," he panted, a proud smile on his face.

"Always," Anna smiled back, before her expression suddenly tightened with dread. She checked her weapon's magazine. "But we have a problem. I'm dangerously low on ammo. I only have two bolts left."

Marche grimaced. A ranged fighter without ammo was a sitting duck in Layer. He glanced around the rugged trail and spotted a thick, incredibly sturdy branch of heavy mountain wood lying among the fallen leaves. He picked it up, testing its weight and balance in his left hand.

Without a word, he stepped over to Anna and held out his cast iron dagger, offering her the hilt.

"Here," Marche said gently. "Take my knife for now. It's better than nothing, and I can use this branch to block and bludgeon. We'll craft more bolts for you once we make camp."

Anna hesitated, knowing how much an Explorer relied on their blade, but she saw the absolute trust in his eyes. She accepted the dagger with a grateful nod. "Thanks, Marche. I'll make these last two shots count."

"We'll get through this," he reassured her.

They pressed onward, their resolve entirely undiminished despite their dwindling resources. But the mountain was far from finished with them.

The narrow path twisted sharply, and as they rounded the bend, a wave of relief washed over them. Nestled in a sunlit, rocky clearing ahead was another wooden cabin, nearly identical to the one in the forest.

But before they could even take a step toward the sanctuary, the earth trembled violently.

Emerging from behind the rocky outcrop surrounding the cabin were two massive Guardian chimeras, their stone-like bodies grinding loudly as they chewed on the mountainside. A deep, thunderous roar echoed off the cliffs, and the Guardians spun around, raising their enormous crab-like pincers in perfect unison.

"Ambush!" Leo yelled.

The team barely dodged the first savage, sweeping strikes. The air filled with the deafening sound of scraping stone and crashing debris.

Marche gripped his thick wooden stick tightly, positioning it defensively. As one of the Guardians brought a pincer crashing down, Marche caught the blow with the wood. The force jarred his injured arm, sending a shockwave of pain through his shoulder, but the sturdy wood refused to yield, holding the beast at bay.

Anna, clutching Marche's cast iron dagger in one hand and her boltgun in the other, waited for the perfect opening. As the second Guardian reared back, she fired one of her precious final bolts directly into its massive yellow eye. The creature staggered violently, crashing heavily onto the rocky ground and shattering into a cascade of lifeless stones.

But their momentary victory was instantly shattered. The sky above darkened with a familiar, terrifying hum. The mosquito chimeras had returned.

Two massive forms descended rapidly from the clouds, their wings beating a frantic rhythm as they dove.

"Watch the sky!" Teitra screamed, throwing up a magical ward just as a sweeping pincer from the remaining Guardian caught her off guard. The blow shattered her ward and knocked her brutally to the ground. She gasped, momentarily stunned, her vision swimming.

Anna pivoted to cover Teitra, but a diving mosquito chimera swooped in, its sharp, multi-jointed claw slashing viciously across Anna's thigh.

A sharp, agonizing cry tore from Anna's lips as the claw sliced deep into her flesh. Blood instantly bloomed, soaking her trousers. She stumbled, falling to one knee, her face paling rapidly from the shock and the sudden, intense pain.

"Anna!" Marche roared. He violently shoved the Guardian back with his stick. "Hold the line! Protect each other!"

Anna gritted her teeth against the blinding pain. As the mosquito circled back for a killing strike, she raised her boltgun, firing her absolute last bolt with lethal precision. It pierced the beast's thorax, sending it crashing into the dirt.

But she was completely defenseless now against the towering Guardian. Desperate, she hurled Marche’s cast iron dagger toward him with all her remaining strength. Marche caught the hilt mid-air. He spun, dodging a devastating pincer strike, and drove the blade deep into a weak spot in the Guardian’s stone armor, toppling it into a crumbling heap.

Leo launched a flurry of perfectly aimed stones at the last mosquito chimera's wing joints, crippling it until it retreated back into the heavy clouds.

The clearing went dead silent, save for the ragged breathing of the team.

Marche dropped his weapons and sprinted to Anna’s side. Ignoring the screaming pain in his own battered ribs, he gently swept her up into his arms. Her head lolled against his chest, her skin incredibly pale.

"We need to get you inside. Now," Marche said, his voice tight with raw panic.

Leo didn't hesitate. He ran to the cabin and pushed the heavy wooden door open with a reckless, desperate shove. The hinges groaned loudly, revealing an interior thick with undisturbed dust and silence. It was an exact mirror of the cabin in the Twisted Forest—simple furnishings, a worn wooden table, a cold hearth—but completely stripped of vines and greenery.

Teitra stepped cautiously inside, her eyes scanning the dark corners. "It's been abandoned for much longer. But it's safe."

Marche quickly and carefully laid Anna down on a makeshift bed in the corner, gently brushing a sweaty strand of blonde hair from her pale face. His breath came in ragged, terrified gasps. The sight of her bleeding so heavily from the deep, jagged cut overwhelmed him, the crushing weight of his responsibility and his love for her colliding into a storm of panic.

"Leo, please," Marche pleaded, his voice cracking completely, tears welling in his blue eyes. "You have to help her. Quickly. She's losing too much blood."

Anna’s eyes fluttered weakly, the excruciating pain stealing her focus. Her gaze locked onto Marche’s, and with trembling fingers, she reached out for him.

Marche grabbed her hand, holding it with a fierce, desperate grip. "You better not leave me, Anna. Do you hear me? Not now. Not ever."

Leo was already moving. He worked with a cold, focused precision, his hands remarkably steady despite the grave urgency. He applied heavy pressure to the wound, rapidly preparing his medicinal salves and bandages.

The room was thick with suffocating tension. Teitra stepped forward, placing a gentle, grounding hand on Marche’s trembling shoulder.

"Marche, please," she soothed, her voice a calm anchor in his storm. "Let Leo work. He is amazing at what he does. Believe in him. And believe in Anna. She is so strong. She wouldn't just give up on you."

Marche swallowed hard, nodding, though his heart still raced uncontrollably. Anna’s grip on his hand tightened one final time before her eyes rolled back. She slipped into unconsciousness, her hand going limp in his grasp.

The sight of her passing out was the final blow. The adrenaline that had been masking Marche’s own severe injuries instantly evaporated. The pain in his bruised ribs and battered muscles flared violently. His vision blurred, the dusty cabin tilting sideways. With a heavy, exhausted sigh, the Explorer lost consciousness, collapsing heavily onto the floor right beside her bed.

Leo and Teitra exchanged a deeply worried glance, but Leo didn't stop moving. The fate of their friends rested entirely in his hands.

The dim light of the cabin flickered as Leo prepared his tools. First, he carefully cleaned Anna's deep wound with a cool, antiseptic solution he had masterfully distilled from the plants in the Endless Plains. He gently wiped away the grim, revealing torn flesh and damaged muscle beneath.

Using a small, razor-sharp scalpel from his kit, he meticulously trimmed away the ragged edges of tissue to prevent the chimera's vile infection from taking hold. His hands moved with a rhythmic, steady grace, entirely mindful of Anna's shallow breaths. He used fine forceps to extract small bits of debris embedded deep in the cut. When the wound was clean, he prepared sterilized sutures. He stitched the gash closed, each knot tight enough to hold but gentle enough to avoid further trauma. Finally, he applied a thick layer of potent, anti-inflammatory herbal salve and wrapped the leg securely in clean linen bandages.

Leo sat back, wiping a bead of sweat from his brow, his expression a heavy mixture of profound relief and exhaustion. "The worst is over," he whispered to Teitra. "Now she just needs rest."

Hours later, the fire's embers cast a soft, warm glow across the worn walls. Anna’s eyes finally fluttered open. The dull, throbbing ache in her leg had sharpened into a relentless pain, but her mind was clear.

She looked down. Her hand was slick with sweat, still clasped tightly in Marche’s grasp. He lay asleep on the floor beside her makeshift bed, his breathing steady, his face bruised and exhausted.

Summoning every ounce of her strength, Anna pushed herself up, wincing sharply as her injured leg shifted. She glanced across the room. In the opposite corner, Teitra and Leo lay curled up together. Teitra rested closely behind the medic, one arm draped highly and protectively over his torso.

A small, tired grin tugged at Anna’s lips. "It's about time," she whispered quietly to herself.

She hobbled to her pack, took a long, grateful drink of water, and slowly lowered herself back down—but this time, she slid onto the floor directly beside Marche. Leaning close, she pressed a gentle, lingering kiss to his bruised cheek.

"You don't need to get so worked up," she murmured softly against his skin. "I wouldn't leave you."

Marche stirred, his blue eyes fluttering open. He met her gaze, a profound, overwhelming relief washing over his features. He didn't speak. He simply opened his arms, and Anna lay her head against his chest, wrapping her arms around him. The warmth of their shared presence was a perfect, quiet sanctuary against the horrors of the mountain.

Unseen in the dim light across the room, Teitra turned her head slightly, watching the couple with a tender smile. She tightened her own hold around Leo’s waist, finding her own quiet comfort as the team finally slipped into a deep, healing sleep.

The next morning, the soft light of dawn filtered through the dusty windowpane. Marche stirred, realizing Anna’s arms were wrapped tightly around him, her good leg draped protectively over his side, anchoring him firmly in place. It was a silent, stubborn declaration that she wasn't going anywhere.

Carefully, he wiggled free, trying not to wake her. As he stood, he heard quiet laughter from across the room. Teitra and Leo were sitting up, exchanging amused glances.

"Finally," Teitra teased gently. "He's free."

"How are you feeling, Marche?" Leo chuckled.

Marche flexed his chest, wincing slightly. "Better. Just bruised ribs. How is she?"

"Healing well," Leo confirmed. "But she won't be walking on her own for a few days. We're calling this place home for a bit."

"Then we rest," Marche agreed.

Marche spent the morning stepping cautiously outside the cabin, gathering dry wood and sturdy sticks. He didn't wander far, his eyes constantly darting back to the small window to check on Anna. Sitting on the porch, he used his knife to meticulously whittle the sticks into fresh, perfectly balanced bolts for her weapon.

But his masterpiece was a long, incredibly sturdy branch of mountain pine. He spent hours stripping the bark, sanding the wood completely smooth, and carving intricate, spiraling patterns along its length. At the very top, curving perfectly to fit a hand, he carefully carved two elegant, intertwined letters: *M* and *A*.

Inside, Teitra and Leo moved quietly, categorizing herbs. Teitra's heart pounded fiercely in her chest. She couldn't hold it back any longer. The near-death experiences of the mountain had stripped away her patience.

"Leo," she began hesitantly, pausing by the table to meet his yellow eyes. "Can we talk? Just for a few minutes?"

Leo looked up, surprise flickering in his gaze. "Of course."

Teitra took a deep, shaky breath, her cheeks flushing as she stepped closer. "I... I love you, Leo," she confessed softly, the words tumbling out in a rush of raw vulnerability. "I have for a long time now."

Leo's expression softened immensely, but his analytical mind quickly took over, trying to compartmentalize the emotional weight. "Teitra, I care for you deeply. More than you know. But right now, my focus has to be entirely on this mission, and keeping us all alive. I want to keep things as they are for now... but I promise, once we're done with Layer, we will explore these feelings together."

Teitra nodded slowly, a bittersweet, understanding smile touching her lips. "I understand. I'll wait. But..." She glanced toward the window, her voice turning playful yet wistful. "How long does Layer even go? Only Paldyne and Melmori knew, and they're long gone.

Maybe things will change sooner than you think. Feelings often show up when you least expect them to."

Leo smiled, a hint of deep embarrassment in his eyes. "You never know. But... I still want you close to me."

"I'd like that too," Teitra whispered, tears welling in her eyes as she reached out to briefly squeeze his hand.

Later that afternoon, Marche brought his finished carving inside. He helped Anna sit up, carefully supporting her weight as they moved outside to sit on two sturdy tree stumps in the fresh air.

"Wait here a moment," Marche smiled, slipping behind the cabin. He returned holding the beautifully handcrafted cane. He presented it to her, the intertwined *M* and *A* gleaming in the sunlight.

Anna's eyes widened in profound surprise and deep gratitude. "Marche... you made this for me?"

He smiled, his gaze filled with a fierce, protective tenderness. "I wanted you to have something to lean on. Something to remind you that I am right here, every step of the way."

She reached out, tracing the carved letters with her thumb. "It's beautiful. Thank you." She pulled him down by his collar, pressing a soft, lingering kiss to his lips, completely oblivious to the world around them.

The next morning, as they prepared to finally leave the cabin, Leo caught Marche's attention, pulling him aside.

"Marche, can we talk?" Leo asked, shifting nervously. "How do you manage your feelings for Anna while on this mission? How do you balance the terrifying danger and the relationship?"

Marche looked over at Anna, who was practicing her balance with the cane, a fond smile breaking across his face. "She gives me something to look forward to, Leo. A reason to push through, to finish this nightmare and get back safely. Honestly? It adds a terrifying amount of stress knowing she could be hurt out here. But that just means I have to be better. Stronger. She is my goal."

Marche turned back to Leo, his tone dropping to a serious, brotherly advice. "Tell Teitra how you really feel. Don't hide behind the mission. What if we never leave this place? Do you really want that regret hanging over your head? Love is easier than you think, Leo. Let it happen."

That night, their final night in the cabin, the space was quiet. Marche lay on his back, Anna resting comfortably atop his chest, both drifting into a peaceful sleep.

In the corner, Teitra sat absorbed in Leo's journal. Leo sat down beside her, the firelight casting warm shadows across his face. They talked for hours about the mysteries of the mountain, but as Leo finally stood up to rest, Teitra reached out, grasping his hand with wide, hopeful eyes.

"You don't have to sleep alone," she offered softly.

Leo looked down at her, Marche's words echoing loudly in his mind. *What if we never leave this place?* He let out a deep, shuddering exhale, dropping his analytical walls completely.

He knelt back down, hanging his head slightly. "I love you, Teitra," he whispered, the absolute truth finally breaking free. "I talked with Marche today. He gave me clarity. A new perspective on all of this. I am so sorry for not being clear yesterday. I'm ready now."

Tears instantly spilled from Teitra's golden eyes. She threw her arms around his neck, burying her face in his shirt to muffle a happy sob. "I love you too, Leo. I was starting to worry."

Leo wrapped his arms around her waist, pulling back just enough to softly cup her cheeks. "I love you as well. I may not be as expressive as those two," he nodded toward Marche and Anna, "so you'll have to be patient with me."

"I have all the patience in the world," Teitra smiled radiantly. They lay down together, their fingers intertwined, finding a profound, newly cemented peace in the dark.

The next morning, they packed their belongings and left the cabin behind. Anna leaned heavily on her intricately carved cane and Marche's shoulder, but her spirit was entirely unbroken. Ahead of them, Leo and Teitra walked hand in hand, their newly forged bond obvious in their constant, affectionate glances.

As they climbed higher into the mountain, the air grew freezing. The rocky path was soon dusted with snow, which quickly thickened into heavy, blinding white drifts.

Suddenly, Teitra pointed upward. "Mosquito chimeras."

The swarm hovered high above, but they didn't dive. They seemed to actively avoid the team, their flight patterns cautious, as if terrified of something further up the mountain.

After hours of grueling, freezing climbing, they finally emerged onto a flat, expansive plateau near the summit. Standing majestically in the center was a massive stone gate, completely sealed, its runes glowing with an icy blue light.

Before they could even approach the threshold, a piercing, terrifying screech shattered the silence.

A colossal creature plummeted from the swirling storm clouds above, crashing onto the plateau with earth-shattering force. It was a bizarre, nightmarish chimera. It possessed the massive, bloated body of a frog, heavily armored by a thick, jagged turtle shell made of solid stone. Enormous, powerful bird wings sprouted from its back, beating the freezing air into a gale, while its feet ended in razor-sharp, eagle-like talons. Its wide, grotesque frog mouth opened to unleash another deafening, eagle-like screech from its eerily human-like face.

"Wait for it to make the first move!" Marche commanded over the howling wind, drawing his dagger. "Then we attack together!"

The beast locked its horrifying eyes on Marche. With a powerful thrust of its wings, it dashed forward, its talons scraping the ice, aiming directly for the Explorer.

The impact of its charge was immense. Marche twisted sharply, narrowly avoiding a crushing blow from its massive jaw. Anna, leaning heavily on her good leg, brought her new wooden cane down hard against the creature's armored shell, the impact sending a reverberating *crack* through the freezing air. She quickly swapped to her boltgun, firing one of her freshly carved bolts directly into the beast's wing joint.

The chimera screeched, flapping wildly to regain its balance, and turned its fury on Anna.

"No you don't!" Teitra yelled, darting forward with her dagger. She slashed aggressively at the creature's exposed leg, drawing a hiss of pain and pulling its attention away from the injured Anna.

From behind a snow-covered boulder, Leo hurled a massive, sharpened stone with his slingshot. The rock struck the beast's human-like eye perfectly. The chimera roared in absolute agony, its movements becoming erratic and uncoordinated.

Seizing the opening, Marche lunged. He drove his dagger into the small, fleshy gap beneath the creature's stone shell. The blade bit deep. The chimera howled, swinging wildly, but Marche rolled beneath the strike. Leo fired another stone, completely shattering the bone in the creature's remaining wing.

With a final, desperate flurry, the team converged. Marche drove his blade into the creature's throat, while Anna and Teitra struck at its vulnerable joints until the massive beast finally collapsed into the snow, dead.

Breathing heavily, their bodies aching from the cold and the fight, the team gathered around the fallen monster.

"We've earned some rest," Marche panted, offering Anna a supportive arm.

After taking a moment to catch their breath and check Anna's bandages, they approached the massive stone gate. The air around it felt heavy, vibrating with ancient magic.

"Teitra," Marche nodded softly. "It's your turn."

Teitra stepped forward, her hand slipping from Leo's for just a moment. Her golden eyes narrowed as she focused on the etched stone. The familiar, ethereal, glowing words shimmered into view, floating in the freezing air exclusively for her to read.

She whispered the ancient phrases in precise, perfect order.

The ground shuddered. The massive stone doors cracked open, releasing a wave of incredibly thick, humid air that instantly melted the snow at their boots. Beyond the threshold lay a terrifying, fog-choked, rotting forest bathed in oppressive heat.

Anna reached out, taking Marche’s hand firmly. Teitra immediately reached back for Leo, their fingers intertwining naturally.

"Together," Marche said, his voice an absolute bedrock of resolve.

The four of them stepped forward as one, leaving the freezing peaks behind to plunge into the rotting, unseen horrors of Layer 4.

CHAPTER 4
The Dark Swamps

The transition from the freezing, windswept peaks of the mountain to the suffocating embrace of the Dark Swamps was jarring. The moment the massive stone doors slammed shut behind them, cutting off the icy air, the team was enveloped in a heavy, oppressive humidity.

Thick, pale fog curled around gnarled, lifeless trees like ghostly serpents. The ground beneath their boots was soft, treacherous, and unpredictable, sucking at their heels with every step. The air tasted heavy, carrying the sharp, acrid tang of decay and stagnant water.

Anna leaned heavily on her intricately carved wooden cane and Marche's strong shoulder. Her injured leg was healing remarkably well under Leo's care, but the uneven, muddy terrain made every movement a grueling effort. Marche kept his arm securely around her waist, acting as her anchor in the blinding mist.

Leo knelt beside a cluster of strange, phosphorescent plants that pulsed with a sickly green light. His yellow eyes were alight with an insatiable curiosity that not even the oppressive swamp could dampen. With extreme care, he plucked a leaf coated in a shimmering, oily substance, holding it up to the dim light filtering through the fog.

"These might have potent medicinal properties," Leo murmured, pulling a small glass vial from his pack to collect a sample.

Teitra shadowed his every movement. Her sharp golden eyes swept the dense fog, her hand resting lightly on the hilt of her cast iron dagger. "I'll keep watch," she said softly, her voice muffled by the heavy air. "This place feels alive, Leo. And not in a good way. It's hiding more than just strange plants."

Leo nodded absentmindedly, dipping a small tin cup into a nearby pool of murky water. He sniffed it cautiously, his brow furrowing, before taking a tiny drop to his tongue. He immediately spat it out, grabbing his weathered parchment. "The water is highly acidic. Yet, clearly, some organisms thrive here. Understanding how they survive this toxicity could be the key to our own survival."

Suddenly, Teitra's fingers tightened white-knuckled around her dagger. "Movement," she hissed, instantly signaling the team to freeze.

From the center of a large, stagnant pool, the surface of the water began to bubble. The team braced for a nightmare, but what emerged was mesmerizingly surreal.

It was a translucent sphere of shimmering, gelatinous slime, pulsing gently with an inner, ethereal light. It supported its heavy body on four delicate, octopus-like tentacles that glided silently over the water's surface. But as it rose higher, the team's breath collectively caught in their throats. Suspended perfectly in the center of the ooze was what appeared to be an infant human child. Its eyes were closed peacefully, its tiny, semi-transparent form curled tightly as if nestled safely within a mother's womb.

As the creature steadied itself on the muddy bank, three more identical beings slid silently from the water behind it, their forms glistening softly in the gloom.

Despite their bizarre, alien appearance, they radiated absolute tranquility. There was no hostility, no predatory hunger. The team instinctively lowered their weapons. The unwritten rule of humanity completely overrode their fear of the unknown—no one was going to strike at something holding a child.

Leo quickly pulled out his journal, his pencil flying across the page. "I'm calling them 'Plasmodials,'" he whispered, completely captivated. "A fitting name for living pools of life."

The team watched in awed silence as the Plasmodials moved with a slow, swaying grace. Their tentacles retracted smoothly, melding back into the acidic water as they slipped away into the foggy depths, leaving only gentle ripples behind.

Marche exchanged a profound look with Anna. "I hope they don't come back anytime soon," he admitted, his voice tight. "Having to fight something like that... hurting it would be devastating."

Teitra leaned over Leo’s shoulder, watching him meticulously sketch the creature. "You know," she smiled warmly, "you named that giant frog-bird back on the mountain, but you never told us what it was called."

Leo glanced up, a faint, genuine smile touching his lips. "I usually wait until I've observed them in detail. But since we've left the mountain, I suppose we won't see another. I called it a 'Testanura,' based on its amphibious features."

Teitra’s eyes sparkled with pure, unfiltered admiration. Leo caught her gaze, a faint flush creeping up his neck. "You always seem so easily amazed by my notes," he pointed out softly.

Teitra chuckled, letting her shoulder brush against his. "It's hard not to be. Layer is full of terrifying things, but the way you understand them makes it all seem like a wonder."

Marche smiled at the exchange, a renewed sense of hope burning in his chest. "With Leo's brilliant mind and Teitra's watchful eyes, we stand a better chance than anyone before us."

The damp, vegetative path soon split, branching into two narrow, treacherous trails winding through the dense marsh.

Marche and Anna approached the fork, scanning the dense fog. Without overthinking it, they chose the right path, where a short, incredibly narrow wooden bridge spanned a wide, bubbling pool of dark acid.

Marche stepped onto the bridge first. The wood was black with rot. He reached back, taking Anna's hand to guide her. She leaned heavily on her cane, stepping carefully onto the weathered planks.

They were exactly halfway across when the bridge let out a horrifying, splintering groan.

"Move!" Marche shouted.

With a sharp, violent crack, the main support beam snapped. The wood completely gave way, plunging toward the lethal, dark water below. Moving entirely on adrenaline, Marche grabbed Anna by the waist, hauling her forward as he threw his own weight toward the far bank. They collided hard with the solid mud, scrambling desperately onto their hands and knees just as the bridge shattered into the acid behind them, instantly beginning to hiss and dissolve.

Leo and Teitra rushed to the edge of the fork on the opposite side, their eyes wide with panic as the last planks sank.

"Are you two okay?!" Teitra shouted across the bubbling expanse.

"We're fine!" Marche called back, panting heavily as he helped Anna sit up.

Leo pointed a stern finger at the dark water separating them. "Do not try to cross that! The acidity is lethal, and we have no idea what's lurking beneath the surface. Stay dry!"

"We'll have to split up!" Anna yelled over the bubbling hiss. "Take the left path! We'll take the right. These trails have to converge eventually!"

Teitra nodded, her golden eyes filled with anxiety. "Stay safe! We will find you!"

With the team separated, the heavy, oppressive silence of the Dark Swamps felt infinitely more terrifying.

Marche and Anna pressed onward along the winding right path. The fog grew so thick it felt like walking through a cloud of wet wool. After a grueling hour, the trail forked again. The first two paths ended abruptly in tangled, thorny thickets and deep, impassable bogs, forcing them to painfully retrace their steps.

But the third path finally opened into a wide, muddy clearing. Dominating the center of the space was a massive, towering stone gate. The ancient stone doors were etched with the familiar, intricate runes, glowing with a faint, pulsing light through the mist.

Anna let out a long, exhausted sigh of relief. "We found it. Thank the Light."

Marche's expression, however, remained tightly guarded. He scanned the foggy perimeter. "We found it, but we can't open it. We need Teitra to read the runes. And with the bridge broken, they have to navigate the long way around."

Anna tightened her grip on her carved cane, leaning her head against his arm. "Then we wait. We hold our ground, and we pray they find their way to us."

Miles away in the dense, twisting labyrinth of the left path, the thick fog clung to Leo and Teitra like a damp shroud.

Suddenly, a harsh, agonizing noise tore through the silence—a sound exactly like two heavy slabs of iron scraping relentlessly against one another.

Teitra froze, her hand instantly drawing her cast iron dagger. "What is that?"

From the dense fog emerged a nightmare. Two towering creatures, easily eight feet tall, lumbered into view. Their bodies were rounded and gelatinous, resembling massive, dark slimes, but they stood upright on thick, scaly reptilian legs. They possessed no arms. Instead, their entire torso split open into an enormous, gaping mouth.

Nested perfectly in the center of the dark void of their mouths was a single, massive, bloodshot eyeball. The lips framing the eye were lined with hundreds of gleaming, razor-sharp metallic teeth.

Every time the creature blinked, its metallic teeth ground together, producing the deafening, metallic screech that rattled the bones.

Teitra's breath hitched, her golden eyes wide. "Leo... these ones are definitely hostile, right?"

Leo didn't hesitate. He whipped his slingshot from his belt, loading a heavy, sharpened stone into the leather pouch. His yellow eyes were sharp, calculating the threat. "No doubt in my mind. Are you ready, Teitra?"

Teitra gripped her dagger so tightly her knuckles turned white. "Ready."

The Nurmyx advanced. Leo drew the band back and fired. The stone flew with lethal velocity, striking the nearest creature directly in its massive eye.

The chimera let out a horrific, metallic shriek of pain, its gelatinous body flailing.

Teitra moved with practiced grace, darting forward to intercept the second chimera. She slashed aggressively, her dagger cutting a deep groove into its slimy exterior, forcing it to stagger back.

But the swamp mud was slick. As Leo loaded a second stone, his boot slipped on a patch of wet moss. He lost his balance for a fraction of a second.

It was all the opening the wounded Nurmyx needed.

The towering creature lunged with terrifying speed. Its massive, metallic-toothed maw snapped violently shut around Leo's left arm.

The sound of shredding flesh and grinding metal echoed through the clearing. A horrific spray of crimson erupted into the fog as the razor-sharp teeth tore straight through muscle, scraping agonizingly against the bone.

Leo let out a raw, agonizing scream, dropping his slingshot as the sheer, blinding pain dropped him to his knees. He clutched his shredded arm, blood pouring through his fingers in a dark, terrifying tide.

Teitra whipped around at the sound of his scream. Time seemed to stop. She saw the man she loved on his knees, his blood staining the swamp floor, the towering monster preparing to strike him again.

Something deep, primal, and entirely terrifying snapped inside the Orator.

The gentle, soft-spoken linguist vanished, completely replaced by an avatar of pure, unadulterated fury. Her breathing grew rapid, her chest heaving. A feral, guttural growl tore from her throat.

"Stay back, Leo!" she screamed, her voice carrying a terrifying, absolute authority.

Leo, dizzy from the blood loss, stumbled backward against a tree, watching in blurred shock as Teitra became a localized hurricane of violence.

She didn't run; she launched herself at the towering chimeras. She darted seamlessly between the two massive beasts, her cast iron dagger flashing in the dim light. She didn't slash defensively. She aimed to butcher. She severed the thick, slimy tendrils holding the first creature's jaw together, driving her blade repeatedly into its fleshy exterior until it howled and collapsed, bleeding dark ooze into the mud.

The second chimera lunged, its metallic teeth snapping inches from her face. Teitra ducked the strike, pivoting on her heel. Using the momentum of its own lunge, she drove her dagger deep, burying the blade to the hilt directly into the center of its massive eyeball.

The Nurmyx shuddered violently, letting out a final, dying screech before collapsing into a pulsing heap of slime and shattered metal.

The clearing went dead silent, save for Teitra's heavy, ragged breathing. She stood over the carcasses, entirely covered in dark ooze and mud.

Then, the adrenaline broke.

She dropped her dagger and spun around. "Leo!"

She rushed to his side, dropping to her knees in the mud. Leo's breathing was terrifyingly shallow, his yellow eyes clouded and unfocused. The blood was flowing far too fast.

"You have to hold on," Teitra pleaded, her hands shaking violently as she pressed them against his shredded arm, trying desperately to stem the bleeding. "Leo, look at me. Stay with me."

"Thank you..." Leo whispered weakly, his voice barely a breath. "You saved me."

"We save each other," she sobbed, panic clawing at her throat.

She realized instantly that pressure wouldn't be enough. Without a second thought, she grabbed the collar of her tunic and violently tore the left sleeve completely off her shirt. The damp, cool air bit at her bare skin, but she didn't care. She wrapped the tough fabric tightly around his bleeding arm, pulling it as hard as she physically could to create a makeshift tourniquet.

"Hold this tight," she commanded, pressing his weak, trembling fingers against the knot.

Leo tried, but his strength was completely failing. His head lolled against the tree trunk.

"No, no, no," Teitra wept. She knew she couldn't treat this. She needed his medical kit. She needed Marche and Anna.

With a surge of desperate, adrenaline-fueled strength, Teitra hauled Leo up. She dragged his right arm over her shoulder and wrapped her own arm tightly around his waist, lifting his dead weight onto her back. He was heavier than she was, the physical toll immediately burning through her muscles, but her resolve was absolute iron. *I will not let him die here.*

She began the agonizing trek through the swamp. The mud sucked relentlessly at her boots. Leo's blood soaked through his bandage, running warm and terrifyingly fast down her bare arm and back. With every step, he grew heavier, his consciousness slipping further away.

"Stay awake, Leo," she gasped, tears streaming down her face. "Tell me about the plants. Tell me about the water. Just keep talking."

But Leo didn't answer. He was completely unconscious.

Finally, through the dense fog, she saw it—the wide clearing. And standing in the center, waiting by the massive stone gate, were Marche and Anna.

Teitra's knees finally buckled. She collapsed onto the moist earth, bringing Leo down as gently as she could.

"Anna! Marche!" Teitra screamed, her voice cracking, completely shattered by exhaustion and terror. "Help! He's dying! He needs you!"

Marche's head snapped up. Seeing the blood covering Teitra and the lifeless form of Leo, he sprinted across the clearing faster than he had ever run in his life, Anna hobbling frantically behind him.

Teitra sat beside Leo, her tears tracing clean paths through the mud on her cheeks. Her chest heaved painfully. She had pushed her body far past its breaking point. She fought the overwhelming urge to close her eyes, but the edges of her vision were already going black.

Through the haze of her fading consciousness, she saw movement in the stagnant water nearby.

Slowly, gracefully, the four Plasmodial creatures emerged from the dark pool.

A sharp gasp escaped Teitra's lips, but she couldn't lift her arms to protect him. The exhaustion finally claimed her. Her eyelids fluttered shut, and she collapsed entirely into the mud beside the man she loved.

When Leo's eyelids finally fluttered open, the blurry, fog-choked canopy of the swamp slowly swam into focus.

The excruciating, blinding pain in his arm was entirely gone. Instead, there was a strange, cool numbness.

He slowly turned his head. Sitting in the mud beside him, her head buried in her hands, her shoulders trembling violently, was Teitra.

"Teitra?" Leo whispered, his voice incredibly hoarse.

She flinched as if struck. Her head snapped up, her golden eyes wide and completely bloodshot from crying. When she saw him looking at her, awake and alive, a profound, heart-shattering sob tore from her throat.

She scrambled to her knees and didn't speak. She threw herself at him, taking his pale face in her bloodstained, mud-caked hands, and pressed a frantic, desperate flood of kisses across his cheeks, his forehead, his jaw, and finally, his lips. It was a chaotic, beautiful outpouring of sheer terror and absolute, consuming relief.

Leo let out a weak, breathy laugh. He lifted his good arm, wrapping it securely around her waist, grounding himself in the incredible warmth of her presence.

As she finally pulled back, resting her forehead against his, Leo's vision cleared completely. He saw Anna and Marche standing a few feet away, their faces etched with a profound, exhausted relief. Behind them loomed the massive stone gate.

"Where am I?" Leo asked softly, brushing a tear from Teitra's cheek. "Did we find the gate?"

"Yes," Teitra wept, a radiant smile breaking through her tears. "We found it. And... we had some help."

Leo looked down at his left arm. Gathered closely around him were the four Plasmodials. From their shimmering, gelatinous bodies extended long, translucent tubes of slime. The tubes were inserted gently, painlessly into his horrific wound, acting like bizarre, living IVs, pumping a glowing, restorative fluid directly into his bloodstream.

The deep, ragged tears in his flesh were closing before his very eyes.

"Thank God," Leo breathed, completely overwhelmed by the miracle of Layer.

With soft, gurgling sounds, the Plasmodials gently withdrew their tubes. Leo flexed his arm. It was fully healed, leaving only a faint string of pink scars where the metallic teeth had pierced him.

But the healing came with a devastating price.

Without hesitation, three of the Plasmodials shot their tubes back out, inserting them directly into the fourth creature. The glowing ooze flowed rapidly through the tubes. Slowly, the fourth Plasmodial began to change. Its beautiful, translucent form darkened, turning a sickly, inky black as it absorbed all the venom, infection, and necrotic tissue from Leo's body.

The creature shuddered. Its body hardened into a brittle, solid mass, and a second later, it crumbled completely into a pile of lifeless, charcoal-like fragments. The tiny infant figure inside was gone.

The team watched in absolute, stunned silence. The chimera had sacrificed its own life to save Leo's.

Before they could fully process the tragedy, the three remaining Plasmodials turned toward Marche, Anna, and Teitra. In a flash, they shot their tubes into the arms of the three standing Explorers.

Anna winced as the slime pierced her skin, but the pain quickly melted into a rush of pure, unadulterated energy.

"What are they doing?" Anna gasped, looking at her arm.

"They're restoring us," Leo said quietly, watching the process with a heavy heart. "They sensed our pain. Our exhaustion. Not everything down here wants to kill us. Some of them... some of them just want to help."

Within minutes, the tubes retracted. The bone-deep exhaustion completely vanished from Marche and Teitra's muscles. Anna's leg still bore its scar, but the lingering ache was entirely erased. They were fully restored.

Leo sat up, pulling his journal from his pack with his newly healed arm. He began to meticulously sketch the Nurmyx that had nearly killed him. "I'm going to name that monster 'Nurmyx,'" he muttered darkly. "I have a feeling I won't be able to get that mouth out of my head anytime soon."

Teitra settled closely beside him, leaning her head on his shoulder. "I'm so grateful to those kind Plasmodials," she whispered, her voice trembling. "I'm so sorry, Leo. I wasn't strong enough to save you myself. I passed out... you would have died if they hadn't shown up."

Leo stopped sketching. He set the journal down, wrapping his arm around her and pulling her tightly against his side. He rested his chin on the top of her fiery red hair.

"Teitra, look at me," Leo said softly, his tone completely devoid of its usual analytical distance. "I saw what you did. You took out two massive chimeras on your own with nothing but a dagger. You fought like a demon to protect me. I could never, ever dream of doing something like that."

He gently cupped her cheek, forcing her to meet his intense yellow eyes. "I am so incredibly proud of you. You are strong. I would have been dead a long time ago if you hadn't been right there beside me."

He leaned down, pressing a tender, lingering kiss to the top of her head. Teitra lowered her gaze, her cheeks flushing a brilliant red, but a profound, healing warmth spread completely through her chest. "Thank you, Leo."

A few feet away, Marche knelt before Anna.

"It's fully closed," Marche noted, inspecting the deep scar on her leg. "But the stitches need to come out before they irritate the new skin."

He pulled his cast iron dagger from his belt. "I'm sorry about this, Anna. It might pinch."

Anna closed her eyes, gripping his shoulder tightly. "Just do it quick."

With practiced, surgical precision, Marche slipped the tip of the blade under the threads, cutting them cleanly and pulling them free. Anna bit her lip, suppressing a hiss of pain, but as the last thread came away, she let out a long sigh of relief.

The team was whole again.

They stood up, gathering what remained of their dried rations. They approached the three surviving Plasmodials, offering the food as a humble gift. The creatures eagerly accepted, absorbing the treats into their shimmering bodies with happy, soft gurgles.

With a final, gentle bounce, the creatures turned and slid back into the dark water, sinking beneath the surface and vanishing into the fog.

"Thank you," Anna whispered to the ripples.

With their strength fully restored, the team turned their attention to the towering stone gate.

"Well?" Leo asked, offering Teitra his hand. "Ready to see what's on the other side of this one?"

Teitra smiled, her golden eyes bright, and slipped her hand securely into his.

Marche reached out, taking Anna's hand, lacing his fingers perfectly through hers. It was their quiet, unbreakable ritual.

Teitra stepped forward, her eyes locking onto the intricate, glowing runes. The ethereal words shimmered into existence, floating in the dense fog. She took a deep breath and recited the ancient incantation.

The swamp ground trembled violently. The massive stone doors groaned, grinding against the earth as they cracked open. A blinding, searing white light poured forth, instantly burning away the damp fog of the swamp.

As the team's eyes adjusted to the brilliance, they peered through the threshold.

The damp, rotting trees were gone. Stretching infinitely before them was an endless, rolling ocean of sand dunes, baking beneath a blazing, unforgiving sun. The heat radiating from the portal was immense, a dry, suffocating furnace that instantly dried the sweat on their skin.

"A desert, huh?" Marche let out a low, impressed whistle. "I've only ever read about these in the archives."

Before they could even take a step toward the heat, a terrifying, metallic screech shattered the quiet of the swamp behind them.

Leo spun around, his blood running cold. Emerging rapidly from the dense fog, completely ignoring the acidic pools, were two more Nurmyx chimeras. Their massive, metallic-toothed mouths were agape, their single yellow eyes locked directly on the team.

"Run!" Teitra screamed, sheer panic sharpening her voice as she violently yanked Leo's arm toward the glowing portal.

They didn't hesitate. Teitra and Leo sprinted forward, leaping blindly through the gate and landing hard on the soft, scorching sand of the desert.

Anna tightened her grip on Marche's hand. They shared a single, adrenaline-fueled glance, and threw themselves through the threshold, crashing into the dunes right beside their friends.

Marche scrambled to his feet, turning back to look through the open portal. The swamp was a nightmare. The two Nurmyx were closing the distance with terrifying speed. The lead chimera lunged for the gap, its massive jaws snapping.

But as it hit the threshold, its heavy, reptilian foot caught the edge of the stone. The beast tripped, tumbling clumsily forward, its upper body crossing the barrier and crashing onto the desert sand.

At that exact second, the magic of the gate reacted.

With a thunderous, earth-shattering crash, the massive stone doors violently slammed shut. The sheer force of the ancient stone completely crushed the midsection of the trapped Nurmyx, instantly severing it in half.

The heavy doors sealed with an absolute, undeniable finality, the runes fading into lifeless stone.

The team sat in the burning sand, panting heavily, staring at the severed, lifeless half of the monster resting at their feet. They were completely cut off from the Dark Swamps, trapped in a scorching, endless wasteland, with only each other to rely on.

CHAPTER 5
A Desolate Desert of Star-like Sands

The thunderous crash of the massive stone doors sealing shut severed the humid, rotting air of the Dark Swamps from their senses, but it did not sever the danger.

The team barely had a moment to process the blinding brilliance of the endless, sun-baked desert stretching out before them. At their feet, half-buried in the scorching, golden sand, was the severed upper torso of the Nurmyx. The gate had completely crushed its lower half, but the horrifying chimera refused to die.

With a sickening, metallic screech, the beast pushed itself up using the sheer muscle of its gaping, tooth-lined maw. Its single, enormous yellow eye snapped wildly toward the team, burning with a relentless, agonizing fury. It began to drag its bleeding, gelatinous torso across the hot sand, leaving a dark, hissing trail in its wake.

Leo instinctively reached for his belt, his yellow eyes widening in sudden, sheer panic. "My slingshot," he gasped, his hands frantically searching his empty pouches. "I left it back in the swamp during the fight! I don't have a weapon!"

Before the panic could set in, Teitra stepped firmly in front of him, her cast iron dagger already drawn. She reached back, placing a fiercely reassuring hand on his chest. "Don't worry, Leo," she said, her voice an anchor of absolute calm. "We will find you something else. Leave this nightmare to us."

Marche drew his dagger, stepping up beside Teitra, while Anna smoothly brought her boltgun to bear, wincing slightly as she shifted her weight on her newly stitched leg. The heat of the desert was an oppressive, suffocating blanket pressing down on their shoulders, but their shared resolve burned infinitely brighter than the sun above them.

"Let's put it out of its misery!" Marche commanded.

The half-Nurmyx lunged forward, its metallic teeth snapping wildly at the air. Anna fired a heavy bolt, the projectile burying itself deep into the creature's tough, slimy hide. It roared, but its momentum carried it forward.

Marche met the charge head-on. He parried a snapping bite with the flat of his cast iron dagger, using his boot to kick the creature's exposed, severed underbelly. As it reeled, Teitra darted to its flank. She moved with a lethal, fluid grace, her blade flashing in the brilliant sunlight as she slashed a deep, blinding arc directly across its massive yellow eye.

The chimera let out an ear-piercing, metallic shriek, thrashing blindly in the sand.

Desperate to help, Leo dropped to his knees, grabbing two massive handfuls of the coarse, scorching sand. He hurled the dirt with all his strength directly into the creature's gaping maw, choking its grinding gears and blinding its remaining senses.

Seizing the opening, Marche leapt forward, driving his dagger downward with both hands. The blade sank deep into the center of the creature's skull. The Nurmyx shuddered violently, its metallic teeth grinding together one final time before it collapsed completely into the soft dune, motionless.

Breathing heavily, the team regrouped. The adrenaline slowly faded, replaced instantly by the crushing, absolute heat of Layer 5.

Marche wiped a thick layer of sweat from his brow, offering his team a proud smile. "We're stronger together. Now, let's get moving before this sun bakes us alive."

Anna nodded, reloading her boltgun with one of the fresh wooden bolts Marche had carved. "That thing was tough—but so are we."

Teitra turned to Leo, a warm, affectionate smile touching her lips. "We'll find you a proper weapon soon. But for now, you did great."

Leo returned the smile, his heart swelling with a profound gratitude. "Thanks. I'm ready for whatever comes next."

The team finally paused to truly take in the vast, alien expanse before them.

Rolling hills of pristine, golden sand stretched endlessly in every direction. The wind carried waves of scorching, suffocating heat that shimmered and distorted the air, turning the horizon into a watery mirage. Sparse vegetation was nearly nonexistent, save for a few hardy, twisted shrubs clinging desperately to the slopes of the dunes. The relentless, artificial sun blazed overhead, its rays so intense that the individual grains of sand sparkled beneath their boots like scattered, golden glass.

"Let's climb that dune," Marche pointed toward the tallest peak of sand in their immediate vicinity. "We need a better vantage point."

The ascent was grueling. The soft sand shifted and gave way beneath their boots, doubling the effort required for every step. When they finally crested the summit, they stood breathless, gazing out over a breathtaking, barren landscape. There were no landmarks, no trees, and no mountains—just an endless, undulating sea of sand meeting a flawless blue sky.

With no compass point to rely on, they chose a direction based entirely on instinct and began to walk.

As they marched, the oppressive heat beat down on them. Teitra, having torn the sleeves from her tunic to save Leo's life in the swamp, walked with her arms completely exposed to the harsh sun and the blowing dust.

Leo glanced sideways at her, a teasing, affectionate grin breaking through his usual stoicism. "I'm sorry you had to ruin your shirt for my arm back there," he said, his yellow eyes warm. "But I have to admit... it's a really good look on you."

Teitra's cheeks flushed a soft, brilliant red that rivaled her hair. She looked away, a genuine smile tugging at her lips. "Thank you," she replied, her voice soft and incredibly warm.

They pressed onward for hours. The desert was entirely silent, save for the soft, rhythmic crunch of their boots and the occasional whisper of the dry wind. The sun remained fixed at its zenith, a frozen, blazing eye that offered no promise of dusk.

Eventually, Teitra stopped, squinting through the shimmering heat haze. "Look. Could be a mirage—or maybe something real."

Rising from the endless dunes in the distance was the faint, jagged outline of a rocky outcrop. It offered the only promise of shade in the entire desolate wasteland.

"Let's head there," Marche said, quickening his pace, a wave of profound relief washing over him. "We'll rest and figure out our next move."

As they finally reached the rocky outcrop, the impossible mechanics of Layer shifted once again.

The sun, which had hung motionless in the sky all day, suddenly began to dim. The brilliant, blinding gold slowly faded into a soft, ethereal silver light. The sun was transforming, right before their eyes, into a massive, radiant moon.

They found a small opening carved into the stone—a shallow cave roughly the size of the cabins they had sheltered in previously. It was a perfect, defensible refuge.

"This looks like a good place to rest," Marche sighed, dropping his heavy pack to the stone floor.

As the sun fully faded into the moon, the oppressive, suffocating heat of the desert vanished, instantly replaced by a biting, freezing chill. But the drop in temperature brought a visual miracle.

The golden-yellow sands stretching out beyond the cave gradually darkened to an almost pitch-black hue. Yet, the crystalline nature of the sand remained. Bathed in the moon's silver glow, the black dunes sparkled with millions of tiny, brilliant points of light. It looked exactly as if the night sky had fallen to the earth. They were standing on the edge of a vast, glittering cosmos.

Anna stepped out of the cave, completely captivated. She wrapped her arms around herself to ward off the freezing wind, her red eyes wide with awe. "It's beautiful. If not for the cold, I could stare at this forever."

Marche stepped up behind her, wrapping his arms around her waist and pulling her back against his chest to share his warmth.

Nearby, Teitra and Leo huddled closely together just inside the cave's mouth, seeking refuge from the biting chill.

Leo looked out at the glittering, star-like sands, then down at Teitra, who was shivering slightly against his side. "Did you want to go out there and see it?" he asked gently.

Teitra looked up at him, her golden eyes shining brighter than the sands outside. "No, I don't need to. I'm entirely happy just sitting right here, holding onto you. I just wish it were a little warmer."

Leo smiled softly, his hands moving to rub her bare upper arms, trying to generate friction against the cold. "Not the best time to lose a layer of clothing, I suppose."

They shared a quiet, intimate laugh, the profound warmth of their newfound bond entirely defeating the chill of the desert night.

Outside, Marche and Anna stood wrapped in each other's arms, looking out over the endless, starry expanse.

"We've been through so much already," Marche murmured thoughtfully, resting his chin on the top of her blonde hair. "I wonder how much farther this world actually goes."

"Paldyne and Melmori only ever mentioned the Endless Plains in their reports," Anna noted, her hands resting over his. "No one on the surface really knows how deep Layer stretches, or how many of these gates there are."

Marche sighed, a heavy, wistful tone in his voice. "What if it just goes on forever, Anna? What if they never found an end?"

Anna turned in his arms, looking up into his blue eyes. "But one thing is absolutely certain, Marche. They found a way back. They survived it, and they built a life. That gives me hope."

Marche smiled, his heart swelling with a fierce, protective love. "These weeks down here have brought out so much in us. Our feelings... even Leo and Teitra's. It hasn't been that long, but it feels like a lifetime. It clarifies what really matters."

"I'm so happy to be going through this with you," Anna whispered, her voice barely a breath against the cold wind. "I just wish we could go back to the city right now. I want to live our lives together. As a family."

Marche’s breath caught in his throat. He looked into her vivid red eyes, seeing the absolute sincerity of her dream. Without hesitation, he leaned down, and they shared a deep, passionate kiss beneath the vast, galaxy-like sky, sealing a promise that they would survive this nightmare and build that life together.

The freezing night eventually surrendered to the searing day. The moon transformed back into the blinding sun, and the cave instantly became a stifling oven.

Sweat beaded on their brows, the oppressive heat forcing them to quickly pack their gear and step out into the brightness.

The moment they emerged from the rocky outcrop, they froze.

Stalking the edge of the clearing, perfectly blending in with the shimmering heat haze, was a pack of terrifying chimeras. They possessed the muscular bodies, heads, and front legs of massive dire wolves. But their back legs were entirely unnatural—they resembled the legs of a large bird, but were made of gleaming, razor-sharp metallic blades. A lethal, scorpion-like tail flicked aggressively behind each of them. Most unsettling of all, their eyes bore the unmistakable shape of a human's, glowing a faint, sinister red, and long, black human beards hung grotesquely from their wolf-like chins.

They were Nighwulfs.

The creatures paced from side to side, their red eyes locked onto the team with a cold, calculating, predatory intelligence.

Anna didn't hesitate. She quickly handed her intricately carved wooden cane to Leo with a confident smirk. "Just until we find you a new weapon. You better not break it."

Leo accepted the sturdy cane, his grip tightening around the wood. He nodded, his yellow eyes narrowing in focus.

Anna loaded a bolt into her boltgun, while Marche and Teitra drew their cast iron daggers.

"They look like pack hunters," Marche whispered, his muscles coiling. "They will try to flank us and attack together. Watch each other's backs. Do not be reckless."

Anna shot him a teasing, sidelong glance. "You don't be reckless either, Explorer. Remember your promise."

Leo stepped up beside Teitra, leveling the cane like a staff. "No one gets hurt today."

"Agreed," Teitra nodded, her gaze fierce.

The Nighwulf pack moved with terrifying, eerie precision. They surged forward silently, their metallic blade-legs slicing through the sand.

Marche took the lead, lunging forward with a calculated strike. He aimed precisely for the joint beneath the lead creature's metallic leg.

The chimera snarled, twisting to counter with its scorpion tail, but Marche ducked the strike, his agility keeping him one step ahead of the beast's lethal arcs.

Anna fired a heavy bolt, the projectile piercing the thick hide of a charging Nighwulf. The beast faltered, howling in pain, but it quickly regrouped with the pack.

Teitra danced through the fray with breathtaking, lethal grace. She intercepted a lunging chimera, her dagger flashing as she slashed deeply across its side. She moved fluidly, weaving between the snapping jaws and slashing blades, countering with deadly precision.

Leo, armed only with the wooden cane, proved to be an absolute tactician. He used the sturdy wood to parry and strike, anticipating the chimeras' movements. When a Nighwulf lunged at his throat, Leo sidestepped gracefully, bringing the heavy wood down in a crushing blow against the creature's exposed flank, entirely unbalancing it.

"Hold the line!" Marche roared as the pack attempted a coordinated pincer movement.

Anna fired again, striking a Nighwulf directly in its glowing red eye. It collapsed, thrashing in the sand. Teitra seized the opening, driving her dagger deep into the exposed throat of a second beast, silencing it instantly. Leo swung his cane, knocking a third chimera into the path of Marche's blade, who finished it with a swift, brutal strike to the heart.

Seeing the tide completely turn, the final Nighwulf hesitated, its survival instinct overriding its hunger. But before it could turn to flee, Anna fired her final bolt, dropping it perfectly into the sand.

The desert went silent. The pack was defeated, and the team hadn't taken a single scratch.

Marche knelt beside the fallen leader of the pack, his blue eyes gleaming with a sudden, brilliant spark of inspiration. He carefully examined the chimera's back legs.

"These blades..." Marche murmured, running his gloved thumb near the razor-sharp edge. "They are incredible. Thinner, sharper, and far longer than anything the blacksmiths back home have ever forged."

He stood up, rummaging through Leo's medical pack until he found a small, heavy-duty hand drill and a screwdriver.

"What are you doing?" Anna asked, watching him work with pure fascination.

"Upgrading our arsenal," Marche grinned.

He worked with master-level precision. He carefully removed two of the longest, sharpest metallic blades from the Nighwulf's legs. Using the drill, he bored precise holes at the base of the chimera metal. Then, taking his own cast iron dagger and Teitra's, he unscrewed the heavy iron blades from their leather-wrapped hilts.

He aligned the Nighwulf blades with the human hilts and secured them tightly. The result was a masterpiece of survival engineering: a weapon with the reach and devastating cutting power of a longsword, but perfectly balanced on the compact, comfortable hilt of an Explorer's dagger.

Next, he turned to Leo's borrowed cane. Using his old iron dagger blade, Marche carved a deep, narrow groove down the side of the sturdy mountain wood. He took a slightly shorter Nighwulf blade, inserted it perfectly into the gap, and secured it with heavy screws. He had transformed the walking stick into a formidable, hidden-blade staff.

Marche handed the sleek, deadly new sword to Teitra, who weighed it in her hand with absolute awe. He handed the bladed cane to Leo.

"Leo," Marche said proudly, "please make a note of these designs. If others see how resourceful we are down here, it might save future explorers."

Leo nodded eagerly, flipping his journal open. "I'll keep the names simple. I'm calling the chimera a 'Nighwulf'."

"Then these," Marche declared, the desert sun catching the lethal edge of his new weapon, "are Nighwulf Swords. And that is the Nighwulf Cane."

"Fitting names for fitting weapons," Teitra smiled, her golden eyes flashing with a renewed, fierce confidence.

Marche spent the next hour cutting thick strips of leather from his and Teitra's heavy vests, fashioning sturdy, cross-body sheaths so they could comfortably carry the long blades on their backs.

They spent the afternoon drilling with their new weapons. Marche and Teitra sparred lightly, the Nighwulf swords singing as they cut through the hot air. Leo adapted quickly, learning to use the hidden edge of his cane to catch and deflect strikes.

Anna sat on a nearby dune, resting her leg, watching Marche move with a mixture of profound admiration and a quiet, lingering longing.

Noticing her gaze, Marche called off the training. He wiped his brow and walked up the dune, dropping to his knees beside her in the sand.

"Don't worry," Marche promised, his voice dropping to a warm, intimate register. "The next thing I make from this world will be just for you. Maybe not even a weapon... maybe some kind of accessory."

Anna’s breath hitched, a vivid, rosy pink flushing her cheeks. Her red eyes widened slightly. "An accessory? Like... a ring?" she teased, though her heart was hammering against her ribs.

Marche let out a soft, deep laugh, his eyes crinkling. "Maybe. But for now, just rest up. We need you strong."

The relentless sun continued to beat down on them the following morning.

As they stretched their aching muscles, Marche cleared his throat, offering the group a sheepish, apologetic smile. "I'm sorry for spending all of yesterday training with these new swords. I didn't mean to stall our progress."

Leo chuckled, exchanging a warm glance with Teitra. "It was entirely necessary, Marche. We don't exactly have a strict deadline. We needed to know how to use them."

"Yeah," Anna chimed in, pushing herself up with a bright grin. "And we had fun doing it. Plus, my leg got some extra rest."

"Though," Leo added, looking out over the endless dunes, "I think we've sat in one place long enough."

Anna practically leapt to her feet, entirely abandoning her cane. "Right! Let's clean up and get going!"

Marche gently grabbed her shoulders, laughing at her sudden burst of energy. "Looks like that leg has healed perfectly. Are you ready to lead the way?"

"More than ready," Anna beamed.

They packed their camp and set off into the shimmering heat. They walked steadily in a single direction all day, the endless ocean of sand offering absolutely no variation or landmarks.

But as evening approached, the sky did not shift into the beautiful, starry silver they had experienced the night before.

The sun dimmed, but the moon that replaced it was a sinister, pulsating blood-red orb. It cast a heavy, horrific crimson hue over the entire desert, turning the golden dunes into a vast, rolling ocean of dark blood.

A heavy, primal pit of dread settled instantly into their stomachs.

Marche smoothly drew his Nighwulf sword from his back sheath. Anna loaded her boltgun. Leo gripped his cane, and Teitra readied her blade.

"Stay sharp," Marche warned, his voice tight.

Suddenly, the desert floor began to violently stir. The crimson sand lifted, swirling and twisting upward as if possessed by a demonic life force. The grains gathered together with a horrifying, grinding sound.

Before their eyes, the sand coalesced into multiple, towering Nighwulf chimeras. They were made entirely of the blood-red sand, their eyes glowing like hot coals within their shifting, granular skulls.

The horde charged.

The battle erupted into a frantic whirlwind of motion and flying grit. Marche parried sweeping, heavy strikes from the sand-beasts, his metallic Nighwulf sword slicing effortlessly through their granular forms. Anna fired bolt after bolt, shattering the creatures' glowing eyes, causing them to instantly destabilize. Leo swung his cane like a master, knocking the beasts off balance, while Teitra danced through the fray, her blade flashing crimson in the moonlight as she struck with lethal grace.

Every time a Sand-Nighwulf fell, it crumbled instantly, dissolving back into the blood-red ocean. But the desert was relentless. The moment one beast vanished, another swirled into existence just feet away.

It was an endless, exhausting war of attrition. Sweat and grit coated their skin as they fought back-to-back, their new weapons the only things keeping them from being swallowed by the dunes.

Just as their muscles began to scream in absolute exhaustion, the blood-red moon began to fade. The deep crimson hue slowly softened, bleeding out into a pale, peaceful silver.

As the moonlight shifted, a haunting, unified chorus of howls rose from the sand beneath their feet. The remaining chimeras wavered, their forms losing cohesion, before they dissolved completely into harmless, sparkling grains of black sand.

Breathing heavily, their chests heaving, the team lowered their weapons. They had survived the blood moon.

Without pausing to camp, terrified the red moon might return, they resumed their march under the silver, galaxy-like glow of the restored night.

"You're a hell of a lot more accurate with that thing than anyone I've ever seen back home," Marche panted, offering Anna an exhausted smile.

"I can hold my own, I suppose," Anna laughed softly, leaning her head against his arm as they walked.

Teitra, walking hand-in-hand with Leo, admired her new sword in the moonlight. "For some reason, I wasn't expecting these to feel so sturdy."

Marche shot her a playful, scolding look over his shoulder. "I used to build all sorts of things back home. I think I know what I'm doing, Teitra."

"I wish we had been able to see that craftsmanship in the city," Leo chuckled.

Marche's expression softened profoundly. "We'll get back someday. I'll show you all the furniture I built for my family's house... and I suppose I'll have to make some new stuff, too." He stole a quiet, loving glance at Anna.

Teitra caught the look instantly. A mischievous, wide grin spread across her face. "We'd love to come visit and have dinner at your brand-new table! Right, Leo?"

"Sure..." Leo answered warily, not seeing the trap.

"Maybe," Teitra called out loudly, "you could even make a couple of cribs for the babies, too!"

Marche, Anna, and Leo stopped dead in their tracks, completely stunned. Teitra just kept walking, her laughter echoing over the dunes.

Marche shook his head, a massive grin breaking across his face. "Aren't you getting a little ahead of yourself there, Orator?"

Anna looked back at him, a sudden, fierce determination in her red eyes. "Well... who knows how long we'll even be down here in Layer.

It could be years. I don't want to wait *too* long to start a life. We're still young enough... so a few years wouldn't kill me."

"A couple years at most!" Teitra cheered from ahead.

Leo dipped his head, his cheeks burning green with profound embarrassment. "What did I do to deserve this?"

The desert rang with their laughter, a beautiful, brilliant sound of hope that entirely shattered the oppressive isolation of the wasteland.

But Layer despised their joy.

Without warning, the silver moon above them began to aggressively swirl, its soft light morphing into a bright, violently pulsating bluish hue.

"That's not normal," Marche warned, the laughter instantly dying in his throat. "Get ready!"

The sands around them erupted. A massive, towering circular wall of sand violently shot up from the earth, completely encircling the team. The barrier rose impossibly high, churning like a solid waterfall of grit, forming a massive, inescapable gladiator arena.

The ground trembled violently. From the opposite side of the arena, a colossal figure stepped effortlessly through the swirling sand wall.

It was a nightmare of ancient engineering. The chimera stood nearly ten feet tall, clad from head to toe in thick, rusted medieval plate armor. Bright, burning yellow eyes glowed menacingly from the horizontal slit of its heavy iron helmet. Every movement it made echoed with the horrifying, grinding sound of massive internal gears.

The Ancient Mech raised its gauntleted hand. Particles of sand floated upward, violently swirling into its palm, solidifying into a massive, heavy broadsword. The blade was unnatural—it rippled and curved with every movement, shifting seamlessly between a solid edge and a liquid flow of razor-sharp sand.

"This is going to be the hardest fight we've ever faced," Marche yelled over the grinding gears, drawing his Nighwulf sword.

With a mechanical roar, the giant charged.

The battle was a desperate, terrifying clash of speed against overwhelming power. Marche lunged, aiming for the massive joints of the chimera's leg armor. He struck hard, but the liquid-sand sword swept down, forcing him to dive frantically out of the way to avoid being cleaved in half.

Anna fired a rapid volley of bolts, aiming directly for the glowing yellow eyes in the helmet's slit. The giant raised its heavy gauntlet, the bolts shattering harmlessly against the rusted steel.

Teitra moved like a shadow, sliding entirely beneath a devastating, wide arc of the giant's sword. She drove her Nighwulf blade upward, finding a rusted seam behind the creature's knee, eliciting a shower of sparks and a grinding mechanical screech.

Leo spun his cane, darting in to jam the hidden blade directly into the exposed gears of the chimera's elbow joint, violently twisting the wood to pry the armor plates apart.

"Keep pressing!" Marche roared. "Don't give it room to swing!"

Moving with flawless, unbreakable teamwork, the four of them overwhelmed the giant's defenses. Marche and Teitra leaped forward in perfect unison, delivering a devastating, cross-slashing strike directly to the chimera's rusted chest plate.

The heavy armor cracked, splintered, and completely shattered. With a final, agonizing groan of dying gears, the colossal beast collapsed into a heap of broken metal and lifeless sand.

Breathing heavily, their muscles screaming, the team lowered their weapons.

But the arena walls did not drop.

The ground beneath them shuddered violently. The circular walls of the arena whipped into a blinding, razor-sharp tornado. The winds howled with terrifying force, the flying sand slicing tiny, agonizing cuts across their exposed skin.

The storm condensed directly over the fallen Mech. Like a reversed hourglass, the sand violently pulled the shattered armor back together, entirely rebuilding the colossal beast. With a mechanical hiss, the yellow eyes ignited once more.

Before the team could even react, two more towering Ancient Mechs stepped through the swirling sand walls, flanking them on both sides.

The odds had tripled.

The sandstorm intensified, the grains forming countless, razor-sharp knives that spun into a deadly, web-like lattice around the team. The blades zipped past them in a chaotic frenzy. Miraculously, they didn't cut flesh. Instead, the sand-knives targeted their gear. With a series of sharp *twangs*, the heavy leather straps holding Marche, Anna, and Teitra's breastplates snapped. The thick aluminum fibers of Leo's vest shredded.

Their protective armor fell away in useless ribbons onto the sand. They were completely exposed, facing three unkillable giants.

"No armor, no excuses," Marche growled, gripping his sword so tightly his knuckles turned white. "We fight as one!"

He lunged at the rebuilt chimera. The giant met his strike with a devastating swing of its liquid-sand sword. The sheer, overwhelming kinetic force of the clash sent a shockwave through the air, throwing Marche violently backward.

He spun through the air, completely helpless.

But as he fell, time seemed to entirely freeze. The roaring wind, the grinding gears, the shouts of his friends—everything went perfectly, absolutely silent.

In that suspended fraction of a second, a calm, impossibly beautiful, and ethereal voice echoed directly inside his mind.

I am Reverie, daughter of Paldyne and Melmori, the voice whispered, carrying the weight of the sky and the depth of the earth. *Forgive the late introduction. But the time has come to unlock your hidden potential as descendants of the Sky Kingdom. We will speak again soon. For now... receive this gift, and survive.*

Time snapped back with the force of a thunderclap.

Marche hit the sand, landing perfectly on his feet. A brilliant, terrifyingly bright blue glow ignited in his eyes.

Raw, chaotic electricity violently exploded from his hands, crackling and arcing down the length of his Nighwulf sword. It wasn't magic; it was absolute power. Without a second of hesitation, Marche slashed the electrified blade through the air toward the nearest Mech.

A massive bolt of blinding lightning arced from the steel, striking the chimera's sand-covered body. The sheer heat of the voltage instantly super-heated the creature, turning its liquid-sand components into brittle, rigid glass. With a shattering roar, the giant exploded into millions of glittering shards.

Seeing his power, the ancient bloodline awakened in the rest of the team.

Anna dropped to her knees on the glowing sand, throwing her hands toward the heavens. A localized, violent torrent of crushing water descended from the cloudless sky, slamming into the second chimera like a tidal wave. The immense weight and pressure of the water completely overwhelmed the rusted gears, rusting the beast solid in seconds before the sheer force crushed its armor flat.

Leo extended his hand, his yellow eyes blazing. A concentrated, burning orb of pure fire ignited in his palm. With a fluid, practiced motion, he tossed the fireball into the air, gripped his cane with both hands, and swung it like a bat. He smashed the fireball perfectly, sending the explosive sphere hurtling into the chest of the final Mech. The resulting detonation of fire and concussive force vaporized the beast entirely.

Teitra stood tall, pressing her hands to her temples as her eyes glowed with a terrifying, wavy purple haze. She didn't strike the shattered remains; she focused her mind outward, sending a massive wave of psychic energy crashing into the swirling sand walls of the arena.

The magical barrier instantly lost its cohesion, collapsing back into the desert floor like a dropped curtain.

The team stood in the center of the silent, moonlit desert, completely surrounded by the shattered glass, rusted metal, and scorched sand of their enemies. Their chests heaved as the raw, elemental power slowly faded from their veins.

Marche looked down at his sword, the final sparks of electricity dancing over the steel. "That... was unlike anything I've ever felt. It feels like a connection to something massive. To our ancestors."

"I felt it too," Anna breathed, looking at her trembling hands. "The water just... responded to me."

"I'm calling mine Bolt Blade," Marche grinned, the adrenaline still rushing.

"Flood," Anna decided.

"Fire Bomb," Leo noted, his scientific mind already analyzing the combustion.

"Mind Melt," Teitra whispered, the purple haze finally leaving her eyes. "I could feel the magic holding the walls together. I just... turned it off."

As they caught their breath, the sands at the far end of the clearing began to violently shift. Rising majestically from beneath the dunes, shedding centuries of dust, was a colossal, ancient stone gate.

"The gate!" Marche said, his voice ringing with awe.

They didn't waste a second. They ran to the towering stone archway. Marche took Anna's hand; Leo took Teitra's.

Teitra focused her golden eyes on the glowing runes. The ethereal words shimmered into existence, and she recited the ancient incantation flawlessly.

The heavy stone doors ground open, releasing a wave of cool, damp air and a blinding white light. Through the threshold, they saw a massive, dark cavern filled with towering, translucent crystals that cast a breathtaking, ethereal glow.

"Let's go," Marche ordered.

But just as they stepped toward the threshold, a deafening, terrifying screech ripped across the desert behind them.

The blue moon violently flashed, morphing instantly into the deep, pulsating, warning-siren red of the blood moon.

Cresting the dunes behind them, mere hundreds of yards away, was an absolute ocean of Nighwulf chimeras. Hundreds of them. Thousands. Their red eyes burned like a forest fire, their metallic blades churning the sand into a massive dust storm as they charged the gate with terrifying, ungodly speed.

"Run!" Marche screamed.

They threw themselves through the glowing portal, their boots slamming hard onto the cold stone floor of the Crystalline Caverns. They scrambled forward, tumbling over each other to clear the threshold.

Outside, the monstrous pack of Nighwulfs hit the steps of the gate.

With an earth-shattering, concussive *BOOM*, the massive stone doors violently slammed shut. The sheer force of the impact shook the cavern ceiling, sending dust raining down on them. The glowing runes on the door flickered wildly, then died completely, plunging the entrance into heavy shadows.

The team lay on the cold stone floor, their hearts hammering against their ribs, gasping for the cool cavern air. Had they been a single second slower, they would have been torn to shreds.

Marche slowly pushed himself up, looking at the terrified but unbroken faces of the people he loved most in the world.

"We're safe," Marche breathed, his eyes hardening with absolute resolve. "For now."

CHAPTER 6
The Crystalline Caverns

The massive stone doors of the gate sealed with a resounding, final *thud*, plunging the team into a dim, glittering twilight.

After the suffocating heat of the desert, the air in the Crystalline Caverns was a shock to their systems. A steady, freezing wind swept through the jagged passages, biting keenly at their skin now that the Ancient Mechs had shredded their heavy leather and aluminum armor. The breeze whistled through the jagged stone, echoing off the thousands of translucent crystals embedded in the walls, creating a faint, eerie, and omnipresent hum.

Surrounded by towering stone walls that seemed to stretch infinitely upward, they found only a single viable path forward. It was a narrow, rocky trail winding alongside a small, subterranean river. The water flowed gently, glowing faintly with a pristine, crystal-clear purity that felt almost entirely alien in a world as corrupted as Layer. Beneath the surface, small, silver-scaled fish darted through the gentle current, completely unaffected by the horrors of the upper tiers.

Marche shivered, his breath pluming in the cold air as he surveyed the serene area. "We should make camp here. Take some time to refresh ourselves before pushing deeper. We're entirely unprotected without our armor."

Leo knelt carefully by the riverbank, pulling out his testing kit. He drew a small sample, watching the liquid meticulously. "The water is nearly perfect," he announced, his yellow eyes wide with relief. "Almost too pure, honestly. But it's safe. It's a welcome reprieve."

Moving with the flawless, silent coordination they had forged over the past five layers, the team immediately divided their tasks.

Marche unstrapped a bundle of dry, sturdy logs he had salvaged from the Twisted Forest, arranging them meticulously in a shallow stone depression. Using a spark from Leo, a crackling fire soon roared to life, casting a warm, life-saving glow against the freezing chill of the cavern.

Nearby, Teitra took a handful of heavy iron nails from Marche's pack. Working gracefully, she hammered a large, heavy canvas cloth across a narrow gap in the cave walls, fashioning a makeshift wind barrier that instantly blocked the biting draft.

Anna, meanwhile, sat by the river's edge. Using a thin, flexible branch, some sturdy thread from Leo's medical kit, and a needle bent perfectly into a hook, she fashioned a makeshift fishing rod. She carefully threaded a bright, plump berry onto the hook and cast it into the crystal-clear water, hoping to catch something fresh to supplement their dwindling, dry rations.

As the fire's warmth began to spread, thawing their frozen limbs, a profound, quiet sense of calm settled over the small camp. For the first time in days, they weren't fighting for their lives.

Marche finished tending the fire, dusting the ash from his hands. He walked over to the riverbank, offering Anna a gentle, weary smile. "Can I help with anything?"

Anna looked up, returning the smile with a breathtaking radiance that completely defied the darkness around them. She handed him the makeshift fishing pole. "Hold this steady," she instructed.

Marche settled down at the river's edge, his eyes focused on the gentle current. He didn't expect her next move.

Without a word of warning, Anna slid behind him. She wrapped her arms tightly around his torso and draped her legs over his lap, pressing her chest flush against his back. She buried her face in the crook of his neck, completely enveloping him in her warmth.

Marche gasped sharply, the sudden, overwhelming intimacy catching him entirely off guard. The freezing chill of the cavern instantly vanished beneath the heat of her embrace.

They both laughed softly, a beautiful, genuine sound echoing off the crystals, as Anna loosened her grip just enough to let him breathe.

She leaned her head gently against his shoulder, her breath ghosting warmly over his skin. "You know," Anna whispered, her voice dropping to a tender, deeply emotional register, "this is the sixth place we've been since coming down the well. That means we've survived five impossible gates. And before every single one of them, there is something we always do." She paused, her fingers gently tracing the line of his jaw. "Except for this last one, when we had to dive through to escape the Nighwulfs. Do you know what that is?"

Marche's cheeks flushed a deep, profound red. The memory of their shared, silent pre-gate ritual—the grounding squeeze of their hands, the desperate, loving kiss—flooded his mind.

"I think I know exactly what you're talking about," Marche murmured, a soft smile tugging at his lips.

He turned his head toward her. In the dim, beautiful glow of the firelight and the shimmering crystals, their eyes met. The heavy, terrifying weight of the Explorer's mantle completely melted away. He wasn't a warrior right now; he was just a man hopelessly in love with the woman holding him.

Without hesitation, Marche leaned in. They shared a deep, passionate kiss, a desperate claiming of the moment that had been stolen from them by the desert. The oppressive, terrifying world of Layer completely faded away, leaving only the soft shimmer of light and the unbreakable warmth between them.

Suddenly, the fishing rod in Marche's hand violently jerked forward.

Marche’s eyes snapped open. He broke the kiss, his reflexes kicking in as the line pulled taut, groaning under the weight of whatever was fighting beneath the surface.

"I've got something!" Marche grunted, carefully reeling the line in to keep the thin thread from snapping.

Anna laughed, a bright, joyous sound of pure elation. She scrambled up, shouting toward the fire. "We got one! Leo! Teitra! Come quick!"

Leo and Teitra hurried over, their faces lighting up with genuine delight as Marche hauled a large, struggling silver fish onto the rocky bank.

Marche grinned up at Anna, his chest heaving with laughter. "Looks like we’re having fresh fish for dinner tonight."

Later, as the fish roasted perfectly over the open flames, the team gathered close around the hearth. The two couples huddled together—Anna resting safely against Marche's side, and Teitra tucked securely under Leo’s arm. They shared stories, passing the warm, flaky meat between them. They spoke softly of their journey, reflecting on the horrors they had faced and the impossible miracles that had kept them alive.

As the fire’s glow slowly dimmed to glowing red embers, the exhaustion of the desert finally claimed them. Safe behind Teitra's wind barrier, they settled down on the stone floor, completely comforted by the closeness of their friends and the promise that they would face tomorrow together.

The next morning, the team advanced cautiously through the winding, dimly lit tunnels. The soft, rhythmic crunch of their boots echoed against the jagged walls.

After an hour of walking, the narrow passage suddenly opened, revealing a vast, staggering chamber that physically took their breath away.

Hundreds of massive, translucent crystals hung from the soaring ceiling like shimmering, frozen chandeliers. Their facets caught the faint, ambient light, scattering it like shattered stars across the walls. But it wasn't the beauty of the room that made their blood run cold.

At the exact center of the vast chamber stood a colossal crystal formation. It was unmistakably, horrifyingly shaped like an anatomically perfect human heart.

Four incredibly thick, tube-like ventricles extended from its massive base, running beneath a semi-translucent, glass-like pathway that spanned the chamber floor. Each ventricle pulsed with a different, vibrant color—red, purple, yellow, and blue—flowing and shimmering like liquid light, pumping raw, elemental energy toward the center.

But the heart itself was not vibrant. It radiated a deep, sickening, pitch-black glow.

An ominous, terrifying aura surrounded the massive formation. It was a palpable, oppressive darkness that physically pressed against their senses. The team felt it keenly—a sensation like thousands of tiny, freezing needles prickling just beneath their skin. It wasn't painful, but it was deeply, fundamentally *wrong*. It made their flesh crawl, as if the heart was a living corruption bleeding sickness into the earth.

Marche exchanged a highly wary glance with Anna, his hand instinctively dropping to the hilt of his electrified Nighwulf sword.

Teitra stepped forward, her golden eyes wide, her voice barely above a terrified whisper. "This place... it's alive with absolute power. But there's something incredibly dark here. Something sick. We can't ignore this."

Leo nodded slowly, his yellow eyes tracking the glowing tubes. "Look at the layout."

Beyond the glass walkway, the chamber branched off. At the far end of the cavern, directly behind the towering, corrupted heart, a massive stone door blended almost seamlessly into the rocky wall, its surface etched with faint, time-worn patterns.

On either side of the crystal heart, two additional doorways stood open, leading into dark, narrow hallways.

Beneath the floor, the four glowing tubes split apart. Two of them—the yellow and blue—disappeared into the side hallways. The other two—the red and purple—curved back toward the entrance they had just come from, leading to unseen chambers nearby.

Suddenly, Teitra gasped. She raised her hand, pointing toward the massive black heart. Shimmering, ethereal words materialized in the air around the corruption, a ghostly dance of ancient text visible only to the Orator.

"There's a message," Teitra said, her voice steadying as she translated the ancient dialect. "It says: *Destroy the corrupted hearts at the vein's ends."*

She turned back to the team, her golden eyes flashing with realization. "These four glowing tubes... they are veins. They must lead to smaller, corrupted hearts feeding this massive one. We need to find them and destroy them to cleanse this chamber."

Marche nodded, his jaw setting with grim resolve. "Then that's our path. We follow the veins, and we end the corruption."

Choosing the closest path, the team followed the glowing red vein back down the entrance corridor, turning into a previously unnoticed side hallway. The faint hum of energy pulsed warmly beneath their boots as they entered a smaller, enclosed chamber.

In the center of the room rested another heart-shaped crystal. It was much smaller than the one in the main room, but it pulsed with a heavy, rhythmic red glow, beating exactly like a living organ.

"Let's see how tough these are," Marche said confidently.

He drew his Nighwulf sword, gripping the hilt with both hands. With a powerful, devastating swing, he brought the heavy, razor-sharp blade crashing down onto the crystal, fully expecting it to shatter.

CLANG!

To Marche's absolute shock, the blade violently bounced off the surface, sending a painful, jarring vibration up his arms. There wasn't a single scratch on the crystal. It was as if the stone was repelled by an invisible, impenetrable magical force.

Teitra's eyes widened as another shimmering word materialized directly above the red heart.

"Wait!" Teitra called out. "It says a single word: *Fire."*

"Fire?" Leo repeated, his scientific mind immediately connecting the dots. He looked down at his own hands. "The elemental gifts Reverie gave us in the desert."

Without hesitation, Leo stepped forward. He closed his eyes, focusing the newfound, ancient magic humming in his veins. A bright, burning orb of pure flame ignited in his palm. With a swift, fluid motion, he tossed the *Fire Bomb* directly at the red crystal.

The orb struck true, erupting in a massive, controlled explosion of heat and concussive force that filled the small chamber with dust.

As the smoke cleared, the team saw a massive, jagged fracture running down the center of the red heart. The rhythmic, beating glow completely dimmed, and the red vein beneath the floor instantly faded into a lifeless, dull gray.

"It worked!" Anna cheered.

They sprinted back to the main chamber. Sure enough, a quarter of the massive, pitch-black heart was now pulsing with a bright, clean red light. The corruption in that section had been purged.

"The colors correspond to our new abilities," Marche realized, his eyes gleaming with hope. "Red for Leo's fire. Blue for Anna's water. Yellow for my lightning. Purple for Teitra's mind."

But their excitement was violently cut short.

Before their eyes, the clean red glow on the massive heart began to fade, rapidly swallowed back up by the aggressive, creeping blackness. Beneath the floor, the red vein slowly began to reignite, pulsing softly once more. It was repairing itself.

"It's on a timer," Marche realized, the gravity of the puzzle crashing over him. "If we do them one by one, the main heart just heals the damage."

He turned to his team, his expression deadly serious. "If we're going to solve this, we have to destroy all four of the smaller hearts at the exact same time. We have to split up."

The chamber went dead silent. The golden rule of Layer was to never separate. But the pulsing, corrupted heart offered no other choice.

"We can do this," Anna said fiercely, gripping her boltgun. "We know exactly what to do."

With absolute, unwavering trust in one another, they quickly assigned their targets. Leo would take the red vein. Marche would take the yellow. Anna would follow the blue, and Teitra would trace the purple.

"When you reach your chamber, count to sixty, then strike with everything you have," Marche commanded. "And then run straight back here."

They split up without delay, sprinting down their respective hallways into the dark.

Leo reached the red chamber, summoning a massive, roaring sphere of fire in his palm. Marche stood before the yellow heart, his Nighwulf sword crackling violently with the chaotic, blinding voltage of his *Bolt Blade*. Anna faced the blue crystal, her hands raised, summoning a swirling, high-pressure torrent of *Flood* water. Teitra closed her eyes before the purple heart, her mind expanding as she channeled a devastating wave of psychic *Mind Melt* energy.

Fifty-eight. Fifty-nine. Sixty.

In perfect, unbroken unison, the four descendants of the Sky Kingdom unleashed their elemental fury.

The cavernous walls shook as the simultaneous impacts resonated through the stone.

Marche sprinted back to the main room, arriving exactly as Anna, Leo, and Teitra burst from their respective hallways.

They skidded to a halt on the glass walkway.

The massive crystal heart was no longer black. It was pulsing wildly with all four colors—red, yellow, blue, and purple—beating at a frantic, terrifying rhythm. With each violent pulse, the entire cavern rattled. Dust rained down from the ceiling, and the hanging crystals chimed in a deafening, chaotic chorus.

The beating grew faster, and faster, until it suddenly... stopped entirely.

A blinding, holy white light violently exploded from the massive heart, illuminating every single jagged corner of the cavern with an almost divine radiance.

Then, the earthquake hit.

The ground bucked and heaved with catastrophic force. The team was thrown to their knees, grabbing desperately onto each other as the very foundations of Layer threatened to tear apart. The roar of grinding stone was deafening.

And just as suddenly as the cataclysm began, it completely ceased.

The brilliant white light instantly snapped out.

The cavern was swallowed in absolute, suffocating, pitch-black darkness. It was a sensory void so profound they couldn't even see the hands holding onto their own arms. A terrifying chill ran down Marche's spine as they knelt in the blinding dark, waiting for a monster to strike from the shadows.

But no attack came.

Slowly, agonizingly, the natural, ambient glow of the cavern's hanging crystals began to flicker back to life, casting a soft, shimmering luminescence over the room.

As their eyes desperately adjusted, the team gasped.

The massive crystal heart had fractured directly down the center. The two enormous, multi-colored segments had been physically pushed apart, leaving a jagged, ten-foot-wide chasm splitting the once-whole formation.

Directly behind the shattered heart, the massive, camouflaged stone door built seamlessly into the rocky wall began to grind open.

Ancient, suffocating dust billowed inward in a thick, choking cloud, swirling around the team and coating their skin in fine grit.

Marche coughed, waving the dust away from his face as he pushed himself up from the floor. He reached down, helping Anna to her feet, his eyes locked on the dark opening that had just revealed itself.

When the air finally cleared, the path beyond the door lay entirely open.

Anna tightened her grip on her boltgun. Leo brushed the dust from his journal, and Teitra raised her Nighwulf sword, her golden eyes sharp and completely fearless.

Marche looked at his companions, his heart swelling with an unbreakable pride. "Let's keep moving," he said firmly, stepping toward the chasm. "No turning back now."

They advanced through the shattered heart and crossed the threshold of the hidden door, finding themselves in a narrow, steeply descending, dimly lit hallway.

At the very end of the corridor stood another massive stone gate. The familiar, intricate runes glowed softly across the doors, casting eerie, dancing shadows on the enclosed walls.

Teitra didn't wait for the command. She stepped forward immediately, her golden eyes focusing sharply on the stone. The shimmering, ethereal words materialized in the air before her.

Taking a deep, steadying breath, Teitra recited the ancient incantation aloud, her voice ringing clear and authoritative in the enclosed space.

The gateway responded instantly. With a loud, magical crackle, blinding light spilled forth from the center seam, flooding the dark hallway.

As the heavy stone doors swung slowly open, the freezing chill of the cavern was instantly washed away by a thick, heavy wave of hot, incredibly humid air.

The team stepped up to the threshold, entirely stunned by the breathtaking scene before them.

They were looking out at a massive, white-sand beach. Violent, towering ocean waves crashed rhythmically onto the shore, the sharp, unmistakable scent of salty sea brine completely filling their lungs. The sky above was a hazy, pale blue, completely devoid of the cavern ceiling.

The team paused, standing on the edge of the stone. The atmosphere was drastically different—oppressive, humid, and heavy. Yet, the crashing waves offered a strange, hypnotic calm. There were no chimeras waiting to ambush them. There were no traps.

Marche let out a long, slow exhale, letting his heavy sword drop to his side. "It’s nice to have it easy for once."

Anna nodded, her red eyes lingering cautiously on the rolling waves. "But it makes you wonder... what exactly could be waiting for us out there?"

"We better be ready for anything," Marche agreed, his blue eyes darkening with an absolute, unyielding resolve.

Before stepping out onto the sand, the team paused, instinctively honoring the ritual they had established.

Marche turned to Anna. He took her hand, pulling her flush against his chest, and pressed a deep, tender kiss to her lips, silently promising to protect her against the crashing tides.

Teitra caught the beautiful moment out of the corner of her eye. She smiled warmly, turning to Leo. She threw her arms around his neck, pulling the completely flustered medic down to mirror the gesture, kissing him soundly.

Hand in hand, hearts steady and their bonds stronger than ever before, the four descendants stepped boldly through the glowing gate, leaving the Crystalline Caverns behind to face the wild, unpredictable oceans of Layer 7.

CHAPTER 7
The Abandoned Archipelago

The heavy stone doors of the Crystalline Caverns ground shut behind them, sealing away the quiet, glowing twilight. In its place, the team was immediately swallowed by a thick, suffocating wall of humid heat and the deafening, rhythmic crash of violent ocean waves.

They stood on a pristine shoreline of powdery white sand. The sharp, unmistakable tang of sea brine and ozone completely filled their lungs. Stretching infinitely out to the horizon was a vast, restless ocean, its surface a deep, churning cobalt blue. Scattered across the violent waters were countless small, jagged islands, creating a sprawling, labyrinthine archipelago.

But it wasn't the ocean that made the team freeze in absolute, horrified awe.

Hanging in the distance, suspended in a shimmering, distorted heat haze just beyond the island chain, was a massive landmass. It was the unmistakable, sprawling silhouette of Orowait—their home.

But it was entirely wrong.

Through the rolling sea spray, they weren't looking at the peaceful, fortified city they had left behind. They were staring at a ghostly, massive mirage frozen in the absolute worst moment of its history.

It was a panoramic vision of the cataclysm. Buildings crumbled like dust. Towering pillars of unnatural orange fire scorched the sky. Though the roar of the ocean drowned out any sound, the team could perfectly make out the tiny, frantic shapes of people scrambling desperately through the streets, their faces etched with pure, unadulterated terror as the apocalyptic shadow of the meteor descended upon them.

Marche's jaw clenched so tightly a muscle ticked in his cheek. His bright blue eyes reflected the ghostly flames of the burning city. "That's Orowait..." he murmured, his voice tight. "But it's not the city we know. It's the Fall."

Anna stepped closer to him, her hand instinctively finding his, her grip crushing. "It looks like hell. They're completely trapped. Scared... and utterly helpless."

Leo stepped up beside them, his yellow eyes meticulously analyzing the impossible physics of the mirage. "We can't reach them. The ocean's currents out there are far too violent for any boat, and the magic of Layer is clearly projecting a memory. It's keeping us separated from the truth."

Teitra's voice was remarkably soft, carrying the reverent, heartbreaking weight of an Orator witnessing history. "We're observers now. We are witnesses to the exact moment that shaped our present, the moment Paldyne and Melmori's worlds collided. We must learn from this."

They stood in silence for a long, heavy minute, the weight of their ancestors' destruction pressing down on their shoulders.

Finally, Marche tore his eyes away from the burning city, looking out at the labyrinth of smaller islands encircling it like a shattered stone necklace.

Between the rocky islets, the violent tide was beginning to dramatically recede. As millions of gallons of water pulled back, narrow, treacherous pathways of wet sand and slick stone emerged from the churning depths, creating temporary bridges connecting the islands.

"The tide is going out," Marche noted, drawing his Nighwulf sword. "That's our path. But those land-bridges won't stay exposed forever. We have to move fast."

They didn't hesitate. Moving with the synchronized grace of seasoned survivors, the team dashed across the first exposed causeway. The ocean currents surged wildly on either side of them, splashing freezing sea spray against their legs, a constant, terrifying threat trying to drag them into the abyss.

The first island they reached was a harsh, jagged outcrop of dark volcanic rock. It was slick with foul-smelling seaweed and razor-sharp barnacles. Small, deep tide pools reflected the hazy, sun-bleached sky, but the team didn't stop to rest.

They sprinted across the next land-bridge just as the waves began to lap dangerously at their boots.

The second island was vastly different—a dense, humid mangrove forest. Gnarled, twisting roots sank deep into the shallow waters, creating natural, impenetrable walls of wet timber. Bright, carnivorous-looking flowers bloomed violently in the undergrowth, and the eerie rustle of unseen creatures echoed through the damp leaves.

Pushing through the dense brush, they finally broke out onto the far beach, crossing one last, wide sandy causeway before collapsing onto a larger, mid-sized island.

This isle was a tropical anomaly. Towering palm trees swayed gently in the humid breeze, casting dappled, dancing shadows over the pristine golden sand. The air was thick with the hum of insects and the sweet scent of blooming flora.

"Let's catch our breath here," Marche panted, resting his hands on his knees.

Anna nodded, leaning her weight lightly against him to rest her newly healed leg.

As they walked slowly down the shoreline, Anna’s red eyes caught a strange shape lying completely motionless in the wet sand near the surf.

"Wait," Anna whispered, holding her hand up.

They approached with extreme caution, weapons drawn.

As they drew near, the creature suddenly stirred. It pushed itself up from the sand with a terrifying, fluid grace.

It was a chimera straight from a mariner's nightmare. It possessed the sleek, muscular upper body and terrifying, dead-eyed head of a massive great white shark. But instead of resting in the water, it stood completely upright on two powerful, heavily muscled humanoid legs. Large, razor-sharp fins jutted backward from its calves, acting as bizarre stabilizers.

Its gaping maw was a cavern of hundreds of jagged, serrated teeth. But the most horrifying detail was the thick, dark crimson blood dripping continuously down its smooth, wet gray skin, staining the white sand beneath its feet.

The Shark-man locked its cold, black eyes onto the team. It possessed a chilling, predatory intelligence.

Before Marche could even issue a command, the ocean surf behind the creature violently parted. Three more identical, blood-soaked shark chimeras stepped silently out of the waves, fanning out with military precision to completely surround the team.

"Keep them away from the water!" Marche roared.

The battle erupted in a blur of motion and flashing elemental magic.

Marche didn't wait for them to lunge. He channeled his ancestral power, his eyes flashing a brilliant, terrifying blue. The raw, chaotic electricity of his *Bolt Blade* violently arced down the length of his Nighwulf sword. He charged the lead chimera, swinging the crackling steel with devastating force.

The beast raised a heavily muscled, finned arm to block the strike, but the moment the electrified steel touched its wet, conductive skin, a massive surge of voltage tore through its body. The chimera let out a garbled, watery shriek, its muscles seizing entirely as it collapsed backward into the boiling surf.

"My turn!" Anna yelled.

She didn't reach for her bolts. She raised her free hand, her red eyes burning. Tapping into her *Flood* ability, she summoned a highly pressurized, geyser-like torrent of water directly from the damp sand beneath the second creature's feet.

The eruption of water hit with the force of a cannon, launching the massive shark chimera completely off balance and into the air. While it was suspended and helpless, Anna whipped her boltgun up and fired a single, lethal shot, piercing it perfectly through the chest.

"Leo, take the right!" Marche shouted over the crashing waves.

Leo was already moving. He spun his Nighwulf cane effortlessly. A bright, searing orb of pure flame ignited in his palm. With a practiced, flawless motion, he tossed the *Fire Bomb* into the air and swung his bladed cane like a bat.

He struck the fireball perfectly. The explosive sphere rocketed across the beach, colliding directly with the third charging shark. The violent, concussive blast of fire and super-heated steam instantly vaporized the moisture on the creature's skin, throwing its charred body violently across the sand.

The pack had been decimated in a matter of seconds.

The fourth and final chimera skidded to a halt. It let out a low, clicking, garbled growl. Its cold, black eyes darted frantically between the shattered remains of its pack and the churning ocean behind it. It was hesitating.

Teitra stepped forward, her golden eyes morphing into a terrifying, wavy purple haze. "I'll put it to sleep," she said coldly, reaching her hand out to channel her *Mind Melt* directly into the creature's consciousness.

But the absolute second her mind connected with the beast's, Teitra let out a blood-curdling scream.

She violently broke the connection, collapsing to her knees in the wet sand. She clutched her head with both hands, her purple eyes wide with an absolute, universe-shattering terror. She was hyperventilating, entirely consumed by a panic that wasn't her own.

"Teitra!" Leo yelled, dropping his cane and sliding to his knees beside her. He grabbed her shoulders. "What's wrong?! What did you do to it?!"

"I... I didn't do anything!" Teitra stammered, her whole body shaking violently as the purple haze faded, returning her eyes to gold. She pointed a trembling finger at the surviving shark chimera.

The beast wasn't looking at them with hunger. Its muscular body was quivering. It was looking at the deep ocean with pure, unadulterated panic.

"The blood on their bodies..." Teitra whispered, her voice cracking, barely audible over the roaring surf. "It isn't from something they ate, Leo. They are injured. They didn't come out of the water to hunt us."

Marche's blood ran completely cold. "What are you saying?"

"They were running away," Teitra choked out, tears of sheer terror spilling over her cheeks.

Before Marche could even process the horrifying implication of an apex predator fleeing for its life, the world shifted.

The deafening, rhythmic roar of the crashing ocean waves simply... stopped.

It was replaced by a suffocating, unnatural, and utterly absolute silence. The team watched in paralyzed horror as the tide began to recede—not slowly, but with a terrifying, violent speed. Millions upon millions of gallons of water were sucked backward into the ocean basin in a matter of seconds. The narrow, sandy pathways connecting the islands were suddenly exposed not as beaches, but as massive, jagged, bottomless canyons of wet stone.

The surviving shark creature let out a pathetic, high-pitched whimper. It dropped to its hands and knees, frantically digging at the dry beach, desperately trying to bury itself in the sand to hide.

Then, the ground beneath the team's feet began to vibrate.

It wasn't the surface-level rumble of a charging chimera. It wasn't the mechanical grinding of the gates shifting. It was a deep, subterranean thrumming that felt like the heartbeat of the world itself.

Far out in the rapidly emptying, massive ocean basin, the dark water began to violently bubble and boil.

A shadow began to rise from the absolute depths. It was a mass of such impossible, incomprehensible scale that it dwarfed the very island they stood on. As the colossal entity breached the surface, it entirely eclipsed the sky, blocking out the sun and plunging Orowait—and the terrified team—into total, suffocating darkness.

Two eyes, glowing with a blinding, ethereal, and terrifyingly ancient white light, pierced through the gloom. They weren't the mindless eyes of a chimera. They were the eyes of a god.

A voice, vibrating with the devastating force of grinding tectonic plates, echoed not in their ears, but directly inside their minds, threatening to split their skulls.

"CHILDREN OF THE SKY. YOU HAVE RETURNED."

Operating entirely on pure, unthinking instinct, Marche stepped firmly in front of Anna, his electrified sword trembling violently in his grip, ready to shield her against a god.

The colossal entity continued to rise, parting the sea like a sheer curtain. As it moved, it displaced the ocean, sending a sheer wall of dark water hundreds of feet high surging directly toward the island.

And then, the world went black.

Chapter 9 The Screaming Wastes

The deafening, earth-shaking *THUD* of the massive obsidian doors slamming shut echoed with a dreadful, absolute finality. It severed them entirely from the roaring ocean of the seventh layer, plunging the four Explorers into a suffocating, pitch-black void.

For a long, agonizing moment, no one dared to breathe. The atmosphere of the eighth layer was heavier than water. It was a blast of freezing, miasmic wind that carried the sharp, metallic sting of ozone intertwined with the cloying, putrid stench of centuries-old decay. It clung to their skin and filled their lungs like a damp, suffocating shroud.

"Leo," Marche whispered, his voice incredibly tight, barely cutting through the oppressive silence. "We need light. Now."

"I'm on it," Leo replied, his breathing shallow.

He didn't reach for his flint, nor did he raise his Nighwulf cane to launch a destructive *Fire Bomb*. Instead, Leo opened his free hand, closing his yellow eyes to focus the newfound, ancient elemental magic humming in his veins. A small, concentrated orb of bright, burning orange flame ignited directly in his palm. It cast long, frantic, dancing shadows across their pale faces. With a gentle, upward push, Leo sent the orb drifting into the air, allowing it to hover a few feet above their heads like a miniature, captive sun.

As the fiery light pushed back the absolute void, the true, profane horror of the eighth layer was finally revealed.

This was no natural subterranean cavern. It was not a sunlit plain, a shimmering desert, or a crystal maze. It was a sprawling, jagged, apocalyptic graveyard where the organic and the artificial had been violently, sadistically fused together and left to rot.

The ground beneath their boots wasn't stone or dirt. They were standing on a treacherous, uneven landscape of shattered, colossal bone structures intertwined with rusted, sparking metallic circuitry. Rivers of thick, viscous black sludge—identical to the tar-like tears that had fallen from Teitra's eyes during her horrific nightmare—sloshed sluggishly through deep, jagged trenches of corroded steel. Twisted spires of warped, jagged metal pierced through a fleshy, diseased-looking canopy far above, resembling the exposed ribcages of long-dead metallic leviathans.

Anna gripped her boltgun so tightly her knuckles turned white, her vivid red eyes wide with sheer disbelief as she scanned the wasteland. "What is this place? It looks like a whole civilization was swallowed alive, chewed up, and spat out."

Marche drew his Nighwulf sword. Responding to his elevated heart rate, the long, lethal blade instinctively hummed to life, crackling faintly with the blue lightning of his *Bolt Blade* ability. "Whatever it was, it didn't die peacefully."

It wasn't just the gruesome sight of the wasteland that set their teeth on edge; it was the sound. A constant, low-frequency, agonizing hum of dying machines vibrated relentlessly through the rusted floorboards and shattered bone.

But woven beneath that mechanical grinding was something infinitely worse. It was a sound like thousands of distant, weeping voices echoing through the miasma.

Teitra stood completely frozen near the sealed obsidian doors, her newly forged sword hanging limply, uselessly at her side.

Her golden eyes were blown wide with terror. The wavy, ethereal purple haze of her *Mind Melt* ability flickered erratically in her vision, unprompted and entirely out of control. Her Orator's mind, trained to connect and understand, was being violently assaulted.

"Do you hear that?" Teitra gasped, her hands flying up to press desperately against her temples as if trying to physically hold her skull together.

"The grinding?" Leo asked, stepping closer to her, his floating fireball illuminating the deep, terrified lines of concern etching his face.

"No," Teitra choked out, her breathing growing ragged as she stared blindly into the sprawling, rusted dark. "The ghosts. They're in the walls... they're in the machines. They're screaming."

The crunch of their boots against the rusted, metallic floor sounded unnaturally loud as the team began to slowly navigate the treacherous landscape. Guided by Leo's floating sun, they picked their way through the jagged valleys of shattered bone and sparking wire.

Every single step required immense focus. The ground was uneven, slick in places with the foul, black sludge that seeped from corroded pipes and pooled in the hollowed-out skulls of whatever massive creatures had once perished here.

Marche took the point, the blue glow of his sword providing a secondary, harsh light. He swept his gaze back and forth, his muscles coiled like springs. "Step exactly where I step," he instructed, his voice a low, commanding rumble. "Some of these metal plates look like they've rusted completely through. We do not want anyone falling into that sludge."

Anna covered their rear, her boltgun raised. She constantly checked their flanks, her eyes darting toward every jagged shadow that flickered at the very edge of Leo's firelight. "It's too quiet," she murmured, stepping carefully over a tangled, pulsing knot of thick, severed cables. "Except for that grinding noise, there's no movement. It feels like the whole layer is holding its breath, just waiting for us to slip."

Leo walked shoulder-to-shoulder with Teitra, keeping a fiercely protective eye on her. He pulled his leather-bound journal from his pack, desperately attempting to find comfort in his usual scientific routine, but his pencil hovered uselessly over the paper. He didn't write a single word.

"I can't even begin to categorize this," Leo admitted, his voice tight with an uncharacteristic, profound frustration. He gestured toward a towering spire of fused spinal column and rebar. "The chimeras we fought before—the Nighwulfs, the Plasmodials, even the Ancient Mechs—they were bizarre, but they had an ecosystem. A functioning biology or mechanics. This... this is an infection. It's a technological rot that's actively feeding on organic matter. It goes against every fundamental law of nature I've ever studied."

Teitra wrapped her arms tightly around herself, shivering violently despite the ambient heat of Leo's floating fire. The purple haze continued to flicker faintly in her eyes. She flinched every few seconds, physically battered by the invisible, psychic static radiating from the corroded walls.

"There is no nature left here, Leo," Teitra whispered, a tear slipping down her cheek. "Only agony."

Marche slowed his pace, glancing back over his broad shoulder. "Are the voices still there, Teitra? Can you focus through the pain? Can you tell what they're saying? Maybe there's a clue, or a warning we can use."

Teitra stopped walking entirely. She looked down at her trembling hands, clenching them into tight fists. A profound, crushing weight settled over her shoulders, heavier than the suffocating air of the wasteland.

"They aren't saying anything, Marche," she wept, her voice finally cracking under the strain. "It's not a language. It's just... raw, unfiltered suffering. It's the sound of thousands of minds that were shattered a long, long time ago, trapped in this metal and sludge. They are just begging for it to end."

She let out a shaky, devastated breath, looking up at her three childhood friends. The terrifying reality of her situation—the nightmare she had foreseen back on the beach—finally crashed over her completely.

"My whole life, I trained to be the Orator," Teitra continued, the tears spilling freely over her lashes. "I studied the ancient runes, the vocal cues of the chimeras, the history of Paldyne and Melmori. My entire job was to be the bridge. To communicate. To understand."

She gestured helplessly at the decaying, apocalyptic world surrounding them.

"But how do you communicate with this?! How do you reason with rot? The Warden of the Tides warned us—the corruption at the core doesn't want to talk. It just wants to consume everything."

Leo stepped closer, his heart breaking as he saw the absolute, crushing defeat in her beautiful golden eyes. "Teitra, don't say that—"

"It's the truth, Leo!" she cried out, her voice echoing mournfully into the dark. "Anna has her *Flood.* Marche has his lightning. You have your fire. You all have massive, destructive weapons to fight this nightmare. But me? If all we have to do down here is burn this place to the ground to save Orowait, then you don't need an Orator. I'm... I'm completely useless."

She dropped her gaze to the rusted floor. The newly forged Nighwulf sword suddenly felt incredibly heavy and foreign strapped to her back. "When we finally end this... if we survive and destroy Layer for good... my entire purpose dies with it. I won't have a place anymore."

Marche sheathed his sword. The crackling electricity died instantly, plunging his side of the formation into shadow. He walked back through the group, his heavy boots ringing on the metal, and stood directly in front of her.

Anna lowered her boltgun, her fierce expression softening into one of deep, empathetic sorrow.

"Teitra, look at me," Marche commanded softly, his blue eyes entirely unwavering. He reached out and placed a large, calloused, fiercely reassuring hand on her shoulder. "You didn't just train to be an Orator. You trained to be part of this team. *Our* team."

Leo stepped up, reaching out to gently take her trembling hand in his. His thumb brushed soothingly across her knuckles. "We didn't bring you down here just to translate ancient rocks for us, Teitra. We brought you because you are *you*. Because you carried me on your back and saved my life in the swamps when I was weaponless and bleeding out. Because your compassion and your heart are the only things keeping us grounded and human in a place like this."

Anna moved to her other side, resting her hand on Teitra's arm. "Marche is right. The monsters might not need an Orator... but we do. We need our friend."

Teitra looked between the three of them. A fresh wave of tears fell, but this time, the crushing, suffocating weight in her chest eased just a fraction. The absolute darkness of the eighth layer was still pressing in around them, but in the center of Leo's firelight, their bond remained a brilliant, unbreakable diamond.

Suddenly, the rusted floorboards beneath their feet gave a violent, jarring shudder.

The low-frequency grinding noise echoing through the cavern pitched up into a deafening, metallic shriek that forced them to cover their ears.

"Weapons up!" Marche roared, ripping his sword back out.

The black sludge in the deep trenches beside them began to bubble and violently churn. From the thick, tar-like muck, the Hollowed Husks began to pull themselves free.

They were a grotesque, profane mockery of life. They were horrifying amalgamations of decaying, human-like corpses fused violently with jagged metal and erratic, glowing circuitry. Their jaws were unhinged, hanging loosely by frayed, sparking cables, and their hollow eye sockets burned with a sickly, corrupted purple light.

Marche didn't hesitate. He stepped squarely in front of Anna, his blade roaring back to life with chaotic blue lightning. "Hold the line!" he shouted, swinging with all his might at the first Husk that lunged over the edge of the trench.

But the blade didn't connect.

The moment Marche's electrified sword passed through the creature's chest, the Husk dissolved entirely into a cloud of digital static and black smoke, completely ignoring the physical blow, only to reform a foot away.

Then, the true attack began.

The Husks didn't swing claws or rusted blades. They opened their unhinged, cable-strewn jaws and released a wave of pure psychic static—a concentrated, weaponized blast of the raw, unfiltered suffering Teitra had felt radiating from the walls.

The impact was entirely mental, but it hit the team with the concussive force of a physical explosion.

Marche dropped to his knees, his sword clattering uselessly against the rusted floor. The cavern vanished completely from his sight.

In his mind, he was thrown back to the freezing peaks of Layer 3. But this time, he was moving through molasses. He was too slow. He watched in absolute, paralyzing horror as the massive stone Guardian chimera brought its enormous pincer crashing down, crushing Anna into the snow. He screamed her name, his throat tearing, crawling through the illusionary frost, choking on the bitter ash of his own guilt.

I was too reckless, a voice hissed directly into his mind, dripping with the Husks' dark, infectious rot. *You promised to protect her, Explorer. And you failed.*

A few feet away, Anna collapsed, clutching the sides of her head as her boltgun slipped from her numb fingers. The psychic wave plunged her into a suffocating nightmare where her *Flood* ability turned against her. The water morphed into boiling, thick blood. She watched Marche sinking into a bottomless pool of black sludge, desperately reaching his hand out for her. But every time she grabbed his fingers and tried to pull him free, he slipped further away, dragged down into the dark. The paralyzing terror of losing him—the one thing keeping her sane in this hell—completely shattered her mental defenses.

Leo stumbled backward, his Nighwulf cane falling from his grasp. His floating *Fire Bomb* sputtered and extinguished instantly, plunging them entirely into the dim, sickly purple light of the Husks' eyes.

Leo was trapped in a hyper-realistic vision of the Dark Swamps. He was watching Teitra bleeding out from the Nurmyx's metallic teeth. His hands were covered in her warm blood. He was frantically applying salves and tying tourniquets, but the wounds kept reopening. His brilliant medical knowledge, his intellect—the things he prided himself on most—were entirely, hopelessly useless. The agonizing fear that he wasn't smart enough to save the woman he loved brought the stoic medic to his knees, weeping uncontrollably.

The three fighters of the team were physically untouched, yet completely incapacitated, drowning in the suffocating depths of their deepest, darkest insecurities.

The Hollowed Husks dragged their rusted, decaying bodies closer. They raised jagged, metallic limbs, preparing to physically execute the paralyzed explorers while their minds were broken.

But Teitra was still standing.

The psychic static that had utterly broken her friends was the exact same suffering she had been hearing since the stone doors closed. She had already felt this despair. She had already hit her lowest point just minutes ago, and her friends had pulled her back from the ledge.

Looking at Leo, Marche, and Anna writhing in agony on the rusted floor, a fierce, undeniable, and entirely beautiful realization ignited within the Orator's heart.

They don't need a sword, she thought, letting her Nighwulf blade fall to the ground. *They need a bridge.*

Teitra closed her eyes. The wavy purple haze of her *Mind Melt* flared brilliantly, illuminating the dark wasteland like a lighthouse beacon. She didn't try to pacify the Husks. She didn't try to understand their rot.

Instead, she pushed her consciousness outward, diving directly into the minds of her team.

She reached Leo first. She crashed through the horrific illusion of the bloody swamp like a falling star, wrapping her mental presence around his panicked mind like a warm, unbreakable embrace.

Leo, look at me! she projected, her psychic voice cutting clearly through the mechanical shrieks of the nightmare. *I am right here. I am whole. Your love saved me in the swamp, and my love will save you now. You are not failing!*

Leo gasped. His yellow eyes snapped open in the real world. The vision shattered like fragile glass, instantly replaced by the awe-inspiring sight of Teitra standing tall amidst the rot, glowing with ethereal, protective power.

Teitra didn't stop. She cast her mind wider, reaching Marche and Anna. They were separated by only a few feet on the rusted floor, but in their nightmares, they felt lightyears apart.

Teitra seized both of their consciousnesses and violently, beautifully forced them together. She became the ultimate conduit for their bond.

She let Marche feel the absolute, unwavering devotion burning deep in Anna's chest. She let Anna feel the fierce, protective fire that drove Marche to survive every single brutal day just to see her smile.

Through Teitra's *Mind Melt*, they didn't just hear each other; they felt the pure, undeniable reality of their love. It was a force so bright, so incredibly solid, that the Husks' dark illusions burned away like morning fog under a midday sun.

"Anna!" Marche gasped, snapping back to reality, his lungs heaving.

"Marche!" Anna cried out. She reached across the rusted floor, locking her hand tightly in his, grounding herself in his warmth.

"The illusions are gone!" Teitra shouted, her voice echoing with a commanding, absolute authority over the grinding wasteland. Her eyes blazed with blinding purple light as she maintained the massive mental shield around them, completely blocking out the psychic static of the layer. "Their minds are just empty rot! Strike their bodies now!"

Freed from their psychological paralysis, the team moved with lethal, perfectly synchronized fury.

Marche pulled Anna to her feet. He snatched his Nighwulf sword from the ground, the blade roaring back to life with blinding blue lightning. With a defiant battle cry, he cleaved straight through the nearest Husk. Without its psychic shield to disperse its form, the raw electricity shattered its circuitry, turning its decaying flesh to ash.

Anna didn't even reach for her boltgun. She raised both hands, her red eyes burning with vengeance as she summoned her *Flood.* A massive, highly pressurized torrent of pure water erupted from the humid air, crashing into three Husks at once. The sheer force washed away their black sludge, exposing their rusted, vulnerable cores.

Leo was already in motion. He spun his cane, summoning a brilliant, roaring *Fire Bomb*. He struck the fiery orb perfectly, sending it hurtling into the drenched Husks. The resulting explosion of super-heated steam and fire obliterated the creatures, scattering their fused metal across the graveyard.

In less than a minute, the physical forms of the Hollowed Husks were entirely destroyed. Without their psychic advantage, they were incredibly frail.

The cavern fell quiet again, save for the distant, dying hum of machinery.

Leo dropped his cane and ran straight to Teitra. As the purple glow faded from her eyes, her knees buckled, utterly exhausted from the immense mental strain of shielding three minds at once.

Leo caught her in his arms, lowering her gently to the floor, holding her tighter than he ever had before.

"You did it," Leo whispered fiercely into her red hair, burying his face against her neck. "Teitra, you saved us. All of us. I couldn't break out of it... but I felt you. I felt you in my mind."

Teitra wrapped her arms around his neck, resting her head on his shoulder. The terrifying fear of being useless was entirely gone, beautifully replaced by the profound, heavy weight of her true purpose.

"I'm the Orator," she said softly, a tired but deeply genuine smile touching her lips. "I speak for us. I couldn't let them silence you."

A few paces away, Marche and Anna were holding onto each other just as tightly. Marche rested his forehead against Anna's, his breathing ragged, but his blue eyes completely clear of the guilt that had plagued him.

"I thought I lost you," Marche whispered, his voice thick with emotion.

"You didn't," Anna replied. She reached up, cupping his bruised face, her red eyes shining with absolute certainty. "Teitra showed me what's in your head, Marche. I felt it. Nothing in this Layer—nothing in this whole world—is stronger than what we have."

She pulled him down for a deep, desperate kiss, fiercely reaffirming the vow they had made on the beach above. They were stronger together, and the horrors of the eighth layer could not break their minds as long as they had each other.

The heavy silence of the Screaming Wastes settled over the team once more, broken only by their ragged breathing. Marche kept his arm wrapped securely around Anna’s waist, while Leo kept Teitra tucked safely against his side. They had survived their first true test in the abyss.

But Layer was never content to let them rest.

A sudden, sharp crackling sound—like shattering glass—echoed through the massive cavern.

The rusted floorboards beneath their boots began to violently vibrate. The deep trenches of black sludge stopped flowing, freezing completely in place.

All around them, the dead, twisted circuitry woven into the metallic bones of the wasteland surged to life. It didn't glow with the vibrant cyan of the Leviathan or the elemental colors of the crystal heart. Instead, every wire, cable, and rusted conduit ignited with a sickly, corrupted, pulsating purple light.

The illumination crawled up the towering spires like a digital infection, bathing the graveyard in a terrifying, bruised hue.

From the pooling sludge, clouds of black, corrupted particle dust began to rise. It swirled and coalesced in the air directly in front of the team, compressing rapidly. It formed a towering, formless shadow that completely blotted out the ambient light of the cavern.

Within the absolute darkness of the shadow's mass, dozens of burning, jagged purple eyes snapped open, glaring down at the four explorers with an ancient, unfathomable hatred.

"A beautiful display," a voice resonated.

It didn't echo through the cavern; it bypassed their ears entirely, vibrating directly against their skulls. The voice was a horrifying chorus of grinding metal and weeping ghosts, overlapping in a chaotic, digital harmony that made their teeth ache.

"Such fragile little threads you weave between your hearts. You call it love. You call it strength."

Marche pushed Anna slightly behind him, gripping his Nighwulf sword with both hands. The blade flared with blue lightning, but the oppressive, god-like weight of the shadow's presence made the electricity sputter and dim.

"Show yourself!" Marche yelled into the dark, refusing to yield an inch of ground.

The thousand-eyed shadow shifted, drifting closer. Its gaze bypassed the Explorer, the Watcher, and the Medic. All of its burning, jagged eyes locked exclusively onto Teitra.

"You think you have found your purpose, little Orator," the entity mocked, its voice dripping with an ancient malice that chilled the blood in their veins. "You think you are the bridge that connects these fractured souls. But a bridge is merely a structure waiting to collapse under the weight of the abyss."

Teitra swallowed hard, her golden eyes wide, but she didn't step back. She squeezed Leo's hand tightly, anchoring herself to the earth. "You're the shadow from the nightmare," she said, her voice trembling but defiant. "You're the rot the Warden warned us about."

"I am the architect of this beautiful silence," the shadow replied, the glowing circuitry around them pulsing rapidly in time with its horrific words. "Your predecessors—the Hero and his Sky Princess—they tried to understand me, too. They thought their bond could cleanse this circuitry. Do you know where they are now? They are the ghosts you hear screaming in the metal beneath your feet."

Anna gasped, her grip tightening painfully on her boltgun. "Paldyne and Melmori... they're the ones trapped in the machines?"

A deep, vibrating laugh rattled their bones.

"Their bodies failed, but I did not let their minds die. I wove them into the very foundation of this layer. They are battery and broadcast. And now, I shall do the exact same to your little party."

The ground violently lurched.

The rusted floor plates between Marche and Anna on the left, and Leo and Teitra on the right, suddenly groaned in agonizing protest. With the shriek of tearing steel, the floor snapped apart.

A massive, bottomless chasm opened up directly in the center of their formation, separating the four friends in an instant. Marche lunged forward to grab Leo's hand, but the gap was already too wide.

"Let us see how strong your precious connections truly are," the shadow hissed. It began to dissolve back into a cloud of swirling, black particles as the cavern walls began to shift, grind, and rearrange themselves like a horrific, metallic puzzle box. "Let us see if the Orator can still speak when she is dying alone in the dark."

The sickly purple light extinguished instantly. The floor beneath them tilted sharply, throwing them off their feet. Screaming each other's names, Marche, Anna, Leo, and Teitra were plunged into the grinding, shifting, pitch-black maze of the eighth layer.

CHAPTER 8
The Leviathan of the Deep

The darkness that swallowed them wasn't the absence of light, but the shadow of a god.

Marche had thrown his arms around Anna, pulling her flush against his chest, bracing his battered body to take the absolute brunt of the crushing wave. He squeezed his eyes shut, waiting for the millions of gallons of dark ocean to obliterate them.

But the crash never came.

Instead, the deafening roar of the surging tide was instantly silenced, replaced by a loud, electric crackle of ozone that made the hair on their arms stand straight up.

Marche slowly opened his eyes. He gasped, his breath hitching in his throat.

The colossal wall of water had not fallen. It was frozen completely in mid-air, suspended directly over their heads by an immense, gravity-defying force. The ocean was peeled back like a massive, liquid curtain, exposing the dark, jagged trench of the sea floor.

From within the suspended, towering wall of water, the colossal entity fully revealed itself.

It was a Leviathan of staggering, incomprehensible proportions, its sheer scale making the rocky islets they had just traversed look like pebbles. Its form was a terrifying, beautiful marriage of organic deep-sea biology and impossibly ancient machinery—far more complex and divine than the Ancient Mechs they had fought in the desert.

Thick, overlapping plates of rusted, dark-blue metal formed its outer carapace, resembling the armored shell of a gargantuan crustacean. Across these massive plates ran intricate, glowing cyan pathways that pulsed like living circuitry, carrying a vibrant, humming energy through its metallic veins. These illuminated lines raced across its body in rhythmic, synchronized patterns, mirroring the steady, multi-colored beating of the massive crystal heart they had cleansed in the caverns above.

Where biological limbs might have been, massive tendrils composed of interwoven steel cables and bioluminescent muscle fiber writhed and coiled in the damp, salty air. Endless waterfalls cascaded from its heavily armored joints, exposing barnacle-encrusted gears the size of city keeps.

Leo stared up at the monstrosity, his scientific mind entirely short-circuiting. He didn't reach for his journal. There were no words to catalog a deity.

The two glowing, ethereal eyes—each one the size of a Watcher's tower—drifted closer, illuminating the terrified faces of the four explorers.

"CHILDREN OF THE SKY. YOU HAVE RETURNED," the voice echoed again.

It didn't speak through the air. The words vibrated directly within their skulls, carrying the heavy, grinding resonance of shifting tectonic plates.

Teitra staggered, her hands flying to her temples. Her golden eyes flashed with a brief surge of her purple *Mind Melt* energy as her Orator's brain desperately tried to process the sheer psychic weight of the Leviathan's voice. Leo immediately caught her by the waist, holding her steady.

"We are not who you think we are," Marche shouted up at the glowing eyes, his voice sounding pitifully small in the vast, empty ocean basin, though he refused to lower his crackling Nighwulf sword. "We are Explorers from Orowait! Who are you?!"

"I AM THE WARDEN OF THE TIDES," the Leviathan hummed, the cyan circuitry on its carapace flashing in time with its words. *"I WAS FORGED BY THE EARTH AND BLESSED BY THE STARS TO GUARD THE ABYSS. I KNOW THE BLOOD IN YOUR VEINS, MARCHE OF OROWAIT. I FELT THE DAUGHTER OF THE SKY AWAKEN HER GIFTS WITHIN YOU IN THE BURNING SANDS. YOU CARRY THE LEGACY OF PALDYNE AND MELMORI."*

Anna's breath caught. She stepped out from behind Marche's protective stance, her red eyes locked on the towering beast. "You knew them? You knew the first Hero?"

"I LET THEM PASS," the Warden replied, a profound, ancient sorrow lacing its psychic tone. *"AS I WILL LET YOU PASS. BUT YOU MUST LOOK UPON YOUR HOME, AND UNDERSTAND THE WEIGHT OF YOUR DESCENT."*

One of the Leviathan's massive, cable-woven tendrils shifted, gesturing toward the horizon.

The team turned their gaze back to the shimmering, ghostly mirage of Orowait. The city was still frozen in its apocalyptic nightmare—buildings shattering, people screaming in silent terror as the fiery meteor descended from the heavens.

"Why are you showing us this?" Leo demanded, his yellow eyes narrowing. "That happened centuries ago. It's just a memory."

"IT IS AN ECHO OF THE PAST," the Leviathan corrected, the gravity of its voice pressing heavily against their chests. *"BUT IT IS ALSO A PROPHECY OF YOUR FUTURE."*

Marche froze, his blood running cold. "What do you mean?"

"THE CORRUPTION YOU CLEANSED IN THE CRYSTAL CAVERNS WAS BUT A FRAGMENT," the Warden explained. *"THE*

TRUE ROT LIES AT THE ABSOLUTE CORE OF LAYER. IT IS RISING. IT IS SICKENING THE CHIMERAS, DRIVING THEM TO FLEE, JUST AS THE HUNTERS OF THE SURF FLED FROM THE DEEP BEFORE YOU TODAY. IF THE CORRUPTION BREACHES THE FINAL GATES, OROWAIT WILL NOT JUST FALL. IT WILL BE CONSUMED. THE CITY ABOVE IS TRAPPED IN THE SHADOW OF ITS OWN ANNIHILATION. YOU ARE THE ONLY LIGHT LEFT IN THE DARK."

The Leviathan slowly raised its massive, armored bulk. As it shifted, the suspended ocean parted entirely, revealing a massive, jagged chasm carved directly into the bedrock of the sea floor.

At the bottom of the trench stood the Eighth Gate.

It was utterly unlike the majestic, glowing stone doors they had passed through before. This gate was forged from jagged, pitch-black obsidian. The runes etched into its surface did not glow with an inviting, ethereal light; they pulsed with a sickly, violent, and jagged crimson energy, bleeding a faint, dark miasma into the surrounding water.

"THE PATH IS OPEN," the Leviathan echoed, its glowing eyes slowly beginning to dim as its massive body began to sink back into the boiling depths. *"DESCEND, CHILDREN OF THE SKY. FIND THE CORE. MEND THE BROKEN WORLD, OR BURN WITH IT."*

The colossal entity slipped entirely beneath the bedrock. With a deafening, thunderous crash, the suspended walls of the ocean slammed back down, filling the basin. But the magic of the Warden held true—a massive, perfectly dry tunnel of air remained parted through the violent sea, leading directly down to the black gate at the bottom of the trench.

The team stood on the edge of the abyss, the deafening roar of the ocean echoing on either side of the invisible barrier.

The reality of their situation crashed down upon them heavier than the water. They weren't just mapping an unknown ecosystem anymore. They weren't just trying to survive. The fate of everyone they had ever known—their families, their friends, the entirety of Orowait—rested entirely on their shoulders.

Leo looked down at the sickly, bleeding runes of the Eighth Gate. His intense yellow eyes shifted from the terrifying abyss back to the frozen, burning mirage of their city on the horizon.

"Then we don't have a choice," Leo said, his voice dropping its usual analytical detachment, replaced entirely by a cold, hardened resolve. He tightened his grip on his bladed cane. "If Orowait is destined to fall, the only way to save our future is to keep going down."

Marche stepped forward. He reached up, unhooking the heavy leather strap of his pack, letting the unnecessary weight drop to the wet sand. He drew his Nighwulf sword, the residual electricity from his *Bolt Blade* humming a low, angry, and protective tune against the damp air.

He reached out, offering his free hand to Anna. His grip was firm, unyielding, and completely devoid of fear.

"We made a promise," Marche said, his blue eyes locking onto hers, cutting straight through the roar of the ocean. "We go down together. Whatever nightmare is waiting for us in the dark, we face it as one."

Anna looked at the man she loved. The fear that had gripped her chest hardened into an unbreakable diamond of resolve. She stepped forward, lacing her fingers perfectly through his. "Together."

Leo turned to Teitra. He didn't say a word. He simply held out his hand. Teitra smiled, a fierce, beautiful spark returning to her golden eyes, and took it tightly.

Side by side, the four Explorers walked down the steep, rocky slope of the ocean trench, the massive walls of water churning violently on either side of them.

They reached the floor of the abyss. The massive obsidian doors of the Eighth Gate loomed over them, radiating a cold, palpable malice.

"Teitra," Marche said softly.

Teitra didn't need to step closer. The corrupted, jagged runes didn't just shimmer in the air; the ethereal words forced themselves into her vision, burning against her mind like hot iron. She winced, squeezing Leo's hand for strength.

Taking a deep, shuddering breath, the Orator spoke the ancient, twisted incantation.

The bedrock screamed. The colossal obsidian doors violently ground open, unleashing a blast of freezing, miasmic air that smelled of absolute decay and forgotten centuries. The abyss beyond offered no light, no ambient glow, and no sky. It was a suffocating, absolute darkness that seemed to physically reach out toward them.

Marche tightened his grip on Anna's hand.

Without looking back at the ocean, the four descendants of the Sky stepped over the threshold.

With a final, earth-shattering *THUD*, the heavy stone doors slammed shut behind them, plunging the team completely into the deep.

CHAPTER 9
The Screaming Wastes

The deafening, earth-shaking *THUD* of the massive obsidian doors slamming shut echoed with a dreadful, absolute finality. It severed them entirely from the roaring ocean of the seventh layer, plunging the four Explorers into a suffocating, pitch-black void.

For a long, agonizing moment, no one dared to breathe. The atmosphere of the eighth layer was heavier than water. It was a blast of freezing, miasmic wind that carried the sharp, metallic sting of ozone intertwined with the cloying, putrid stench of centuries-old decay. It clung to their skin and filled their lungs like a damp, suffocating shroud.

"Leo," Marche whispered, his voice incredibly tight, barely cutting through the oppressive silence. "We need light. Now."

"I'm on it," Leo replied, his breathing shallow.

He didn't reach for his flint, nor did he raise his Nighwulf cane to launch a destructive *Fire Bomb*. Instead, Leo opened his free hand, closing his yellow eyes to focus the newfound, ancient elemental magic humming in his veins. A small, concentrated orb of bright, burning orange flame ignited directly in his palm. It cast long, frantic, dancing shadows across their pale faces. With a gentle, upward push, Leo sent the orb drifting into the air, allowing it to hover a few feet above their heads like a miniature, captive sun.

As the fiery light pushed back the absolute void, the true, profane horror of the eighth layer was finally revealed.

This was no natural subterranean cavern. It was not a sunlit plain, a shimmering desert, or a crystal maze. It was a sprawling, jagged, apocalyptic graveyard where the organic and the artificial had been violently, sadistically fused together and left to rot.

The ground beneath their boots wasn't stone or dirt. They were standing on a treacherous, uneven landscape of shattered, colossal bone structures intertwined with rusted, sparking metallic circuitry. Rivers of thick, viscous black sludge—identical to the tar-like tears that had fallen from Teitra's eyes during her horrific nightmare—sloshed sluggishly through deep, jagged trenches of corroded steel. Twisted spires of warped, jagged metal pierced through a fleshy, diseased-looking canopy far above, resembling the exposed ribcages of long-dead metallic leviathans.

Anna gripped her boltgun so tightly her knuckles turned white, her vivid red eyes wide with sheer disbelief as she scanned the wasteland. "What is this place? It looks like a whole civilization was swallowed alive, chewed up, and spat out."

Marche drew his Nighwulf sword. Responding to his elevated heart rate, the long, lethal blade instinctively hummed to life, crackling faintly with the blue lightning of his *Bolt Blade* ability. "Whatever it was, it didn't die peacefully."

It wasn't just the gruesome sight of the wasteland that set their teeth on edge; it was the sound. A constant, low-frequency, agonizing hum of dying machines vibrated relentlessly through the rusted floorboards and shattered bone.

But woven beneath that mechanical grinding was something infinitely worse. It was a sound like thousands of distant, weeping voices echoing through the miasma.

Teitra stood completely frozen near the sealed obsidian doors, her newly forged sword hanging limply, uselessly at her side.

Her golden eyes were blown wide with terror. The wavy, ethereal purple haze of her *Mind Melt* ability flickered erratically in her vision, unprompted and entirely out of control. Her Orator's mind, trained to connect and understand, was being violently assaulted.

"Do you hear that?" Teitra gasped, her hands flying up to press desperately against her temples as if trying to physically hold her skull together.

"The grinding?" Leo asked, stepping closer to her, his floating fireball illuminating the deep, terrified lines of concern etching his face.

"No," Teitra choked out, her breathing growing ragged as she stared blindly into the sprawling, rusted dark. "The ghosts. They're in the walls... they're in the machines. They're screaming."

The crunch of their boots against the rusted, metallic floor sounded unnaturally loud as the team began to slowly navigate the treacherous landscape. Guided by Leo's floating sun, they picked their way through the jagged valleys of shattered bone and sparking wire.

Every single step required immense focus. The ground was uneven, slick in places with the foul, black sludge that seeped from corroded pipes and pooled in the hollowed-out skulls of whatever massive creatures had once perished here.

Marche took the point, the blue glow of his sword providing a secondary, harsh light. He swept his gaze back and forth, his muscles coiled like springs. "Step exactly where I step," he instructed, his voice a low, commanding rumble. "Some of these metal plates look like they've rusted completely through. We do not want anyone falling into that sludge."

Anna covered their rear, her boltgun raised. She constantly checked their flanks, her eyes darting toward every jagged shadow that flickered at the very edge of Leo's firelight. "It's too quiet," she murmured, stepping carefully over a tangled, pulsing knot of thick, severed cables. "Except for that grinding noise, there's no movement.

It feels like the whole layer is holding its breath, just waiting for us to slip."

Leo walked shoulder-to-shoulder with Teitra, keeping a fiercely protective eye on her. He pulled his leather-bound journal from his pack, desperately attempting to find comfort in his usual scientific routine, but his pencil hovered uselessly over the paper. He didn't write a single word.

"I can't even begin to categorize this," Leo admitted, his voice tight with an uncharacteristic, profound frustration. He gestured toward a towering spire of fused spinal column and rebar. "The chimeras we fought before—the Nighwulfs, the Plasmodials, even the Ancient Mechs—they were bizarre, but they had an ecosystem. A functioning biology or mechanics. This... this is an infection. It's a technological rot that's actively feeding on organic matter. It goes against every fundamental law of nature I've ever studied."

Teitra wrapped her arms tightly around herself, shivering violently despite the ambient heat of Leo's floating fire. The purple haze continued to flicker faintly in her eyes. She flinched every few seconds, physically battered by the invisible, psychic static radiating from the corroded walls.

"There is no nature left here, Leo," Teitra whispered, a tear slipping down her cheek. "Only agony."

Marche slowed his pace, glancing back over his broad shoulder. "Are the voices still there, Teitra? Can you focus through the pain? Can you tell what they're saying? Maybe there's a clue, or a warning we can use."

Teitra stopped walking entirely. She looked down at her trembling hands, clenching them into tight fists. A profound, crushing weight settled over her shoulders, heavier than the suffocating air of the wasteland.

"They aren't saying anything, Marche," she wept, her voice finally cracking under the strain. "It's not a language. It's just... raw, unfiltered suffering. It’s the sound of thousands of minds that were shattered a long, long time ago, trapped in this metal and sludge. They are just begging for it to end."

She let out a shaky, devastated breath, looking up at her three childhood friends. The terrifying reality of her situation—the nightmare she had foreseen back on the beach—finally crashed over her completely.

"My whole life, I trained to be the Orator," Teitra continued, the tears spilling freely over her lashes. "I studied the ancient runes, the vocal cues of the chimeras, the history of Paldyne and Melmori. My entire job was to be the bridge. To communicate. To understand."

She gestured helplessly at the decaying, apocalyptic world surrounding them.

"But how do you communicate with this?! How do you reason with rot? The Warden of the Tides warned us—the corruption at the core doesn't want to talk. It just wants to consume everything."

Leo stepped closer, his heart breaking as he saw the absolute, crushing defeat in her beautiful golden eyes. "Teitra, don't say that—"

"It's the truth, Leo!" she cried out, her voice echoing mournfully into the dark. "Anna has her *Flood.* Marche has his lightning. You have your fire. You all have massive, destructive weapons to fight this nightmare. But me? If all we have to do down here is burn this place to the ground to save Orowait, then you don't need an Orator. I'm... I'm completely useless."

She dropped her gaze to the rusted floor. The newly forged Nighwulf sword suddenly felt incredibly heavy and foreign strapped to her back. "When we finally end this... if we survive and destroy Layer for good... my entire purpose dies with it. I won't have a place anymore."

Marche sheathed his sword. The crackling electricity died instantly, plunging his side of the formation into shadow. He walked back through the group, his heavy boots ringing on the metal, and stood directly in front of her.

Anna lowered her boltgun, her fierce expression softening into one of deep, empathetic sorrow.

"Teitra, look at me," Marche commanded softly, his blue eyes entirely unwavering. He reached out and placed a large, calloused, fiercely reassuring hand on her shoulder. "You didn't just train to be an Orator. You trained to be part of this team. *Our* team."

Leo stepped up, reaching out to gently take her trembling hand in his. His thumb brushed soothingly across her knuckles. "We didn't bring you down here just to translate ancient rocks for us, Teitra. We brought you because you are *you*. Because you carried me on your back and saved my life in the swamps when I was weaponless and bleeding out. Because your compassion and your heart are the only things keeping us grounded and human in a place like this."

Anna moved to her other side, resting her hand on Teitra's arm. "Marche is right. The monsters might not need an Orator... but we do. We need our friend."

Teitra looked between the three of them. A fresh wave of tears fell, but this time, the crushing, suffocating weight in her chest eased just a fraction. The absolute darkness of the eighth layer was still pressing in around them, but in the center of Leo's firelight, their bond remained a brilliant, unbreakable diamond.

Suddenly, the rusted floorboards beneath their feet gave a violent, jarring shudder.

The low-frequency grinding noise echoing through the cavern pitched up into a deafening, metallic shriek that forced them to cover their ears.

"Weapons up!" Marche roared, ripping his sword back out.

The black sludge in the deep trenches beside them began to bubble and violently churn. From the thick, tar-like muck, the Hollowed Husks began to pull themselves free.

They were a grotesque, profane mockery of life. They were horrifying amalgamations of decaying, human-like corpses fused violently with jagged metal and erratic, glowing circuitry. Their jaws were unhinged, hanging loosely by frayed, sparking cables, and their hollow eye sockets burned with a sickly, corrupted purple light.

Marche didn't hesitate. He stepped squarely in front of Anna, his blade roaring back to life with chaotic blue lightning. "Hold the line!" he shouted, swinging with all his might at the first Husk that lunged over the edge of the trench.

But the blade didn't connect.

The moment Marche's electrified sword passed through the creature's chest, the Husk dissolved entirely into a cloud of digital static and black smoke, completely ignoring the physical blow, only to reform a foot away.

Then, the true attack began.

The Husks didn't swing claws or rusted blades. They opened their unhinged, cable-strewn jaws and released a wave of pure psychic static—a concentrated, weaponized blast of the raw, unfiltered suffering Teitra had felt radiating from the walls.

The impact was entirely mental, but it hit the team with the concussive force of a physical explosion.

Marche dropped to his knees, his sword clattering uselessly against the rusted floor. The cavern vanished completely from his sight.

In his mind, he was thrown back to the freezing peaks of Layer 3. But this time, he was moving through molasses. He was too slow. He watched in absolute, paralyzing horror as the massive stone Guardian chimera brought its enormous pincer crashing down, crushing Anna into the snow. He screamed her name, his throat tearing, crawling through the illusionary frost, choking on the bitter ash of his own guilt.

I was too reckless, a voice hissed directly into his mind, dripping with the Husks' dark, infectious rot. *You promised to protect her, Explorer. And you failed.*

A few feet away, Anna collapsed, clutching the sides of her head as her boltgun slipped from her numb fingers. The psychic wave plunged her into a suffocating nightmare where her *Flood* ability turned against her. The water morphed into boiling, thick blood. She watched Marche sinking into a bottomless pool of black sludge, desperately reaching his hand out for her. But every time she grabbed his fingers and tried to pull him free, he slipped further away, dragged down into the dark. The paralyzing terror of losing him—the one thing keeping her sane in this hell—completely shattered her mental defenses.

Leo stumbled backward, his Nighwulf cane falling from his grasp. His floating *Fire Bomb* sputtered and extinguished instantly, plunging them entirely into the dim, sickly purple light of the Husks' eyes.

Leo was trapped in a hyper-realistic vision of the Dark Swamps. He was watching Teitra bleeding out from the Nurmyx's metallic teeth. His hands were covered in her warm blood. He was frantically applying salves and tying tourniquets, but the wounds kept reopening. His brilliant medical knowledge, his intellect—the things he prided himself on most—were entirely, hopelessly useless. The agonizing fear that he wasn't smart enough to save the woman he loved brought the stoic medic to his knees, weeping uncontrollably.

The three fighters of the team were physically untouched, yet completely incapacitated, drowning in the suffocating depths of their deepest, darkest insecurities.

The Hollowed Husks dragged their rusted, decaying bodies closer. They raised jagged, metallic limbs, preparing to physically execute the paralyzed explorers while their minds were broken.

But Teitra was still standing.

The psychic static that had utterly broken her friends was the exact same suffering she had been hearing since the stone doors closed. She had already felt this despair. She had already hit her lowest point just minutes ago, and her friends had pulled her back from the ledge.

Looking at Leo, Marche, and Anna writhing in agony on the rusted floor, a fierce, undeniable, and entirely beautiful realization ignited within the Orator's heart.

They don't need a sword, she thought, letting her Nighwulf blade fall to the ground. *They need a bridge.*

Teitra closed her eyes. The wavy purple haze of her *Mind Melt* flared brilliantly, illuminating the dark wasteland like a lighthouse beacon. She didn't try to pacify the Husks. She didn't try to understand their rot.

Instead, she pushed her consciousness outward, diving directly into the minds of her team.

She reached Leo first. She crashed through the horrific illusion of the bloody swamp like a falling star, wrapping her mental presence around his panicked mind like a warm, unbreakable embrace.

Leo, look at me! she projected, her psychic voice cutting clearly through the mechanical shrieks of the nightmare. *I am right here. I am whole. Your love saved me in the swamp, and my love will save you now. You are not failing!*

Leo gasped. His yellow eyes snapped open in the real world. The vision shattered like fragile glass, instantly replaced by the awe-inspiring sight of Teitra standing tall amidst the rot, glowing with ethereal, protective power.

Teitra didn't stop. She cast her mind wider, reaching Marche and Anna. They were separated by only a few feet on the rusted floor, but in their nightmares, they felt lightyears apart.

Teitra seized both of their consciousnesses and violently, beautifully forced them together. She became the ultimate conduit for their bond.

She let Marche feel the absolute, unwavering devotion burning deep in Anna's chest. She let Anna feel the fierce, protective fire that drove Marche to survive every single brutal day just to see her smile.

Through Teitra's *Mind Melt*, they didn't just hear each other; they felt the pure, undeniable reality of their love. It was a force so bright, so incredibly solid, that the Husks' dark illusions burned away like morning fog under a midday sun.

"Anna!" Marche gasped, snapping back to reality, his lungs heaving.

"Marche!" Anna cried out. She reached across the rusted floor, locking her hand tightly in his, grounding herself in his warmth.

"The illusions are gone!" Teitra shouted, her voice echoing with a commanding, absolute authority over the grinding wasteland. Her eyes blazed with blinding purple light as she maintained the massive mental shield around them, completely blocking out the psychic static of the layer. "Their minds are just empty rot! Strike their bodies now!"

Freed from their psychological paralysis, the team moved with lethal, perfectly synchronized fury.

Marche pulled Anna to her feet. He snatched his Nighwulf sword from the ground, the blade roaring back to life with blinding blue lightning. With a defiant battle cry, he cleaved straight through the nearest Husk. Without its psychic shield to disperse its form, the raw electricity shattered its circuitry, turning its decaying flesh to ash.

Anna didn't even reach for her boltgun. She raised both hands, her red eyes burning with vengeance as she summoned her *Flood*. A massive, highly pressurized torrent of pure water erupted from the humid air, crashing into three Husks at once. The sheer force washed away their black sludge, exposing their rusted, vulnerable cores.

Leo was already in motion. He spun his cane, summoning a brilliant, roaring *Fire Bomb*. He struck the fiery orb perfectly, sending it hurtling into the drenched Husks. The resulting explosion of super-heated steam and fire obliterated the creatures, scattering their fused metal across the graveyard.

In less than a minute, the physical forms of the Hollowed Husks were entirely destroyed. Without their psychic advantage, they were incredibly frail.

The cavern fell quiet again, save for the distant, dying hum of machinery.

Leo dropped his cane and ran straight to Teitra. As the purple glow faded from her eyes, her knees buckled, utterly exhausted from the immense mental strain of shielding three minds at once.

Leo caught her in his arms, lowering her gently to the floor, holding her tighter than he ever had before.

"You did it," Leo whispered fiercely into her red hair, burying his face against her neck. "Teitra, you saved us. All of us. I couldn't break out of it... but I felt you. I felt you in my mind."

Teitra wrapped her arms around his neck, resting her head on his shoulder. The terrifying fear of being useless was entirely gone, beautifully replaced by the profound, heavy weight of her true purpose.

"I'm the Orator," she said softly, a tired but deeply genuine smile touching her lips. "I speak for us. I couldn't let them silence you."

A few paces away, Marche and Anna were holding onto each other just as tightly. Marche rested his forehead against Anna's, his breathing ragged, but his blue eyes completely clear of the guilt that had plagued him.

"I thought I lost you," Marche whispered, his voice thick with emotion.

"You didn't," Anna replied. She reached up, cupping his bruised face, her red eyes shining with absolute certainty. "Teitra showed me what's in your head, Marche. I felt it. Nothing in this Layer—nothing in this whole world—is stronger than what we have."

She pulled him down for a deep, desperate kiss, fiercely reaffirming the vow they had made on the beach above. They were stronger together, and the horrors of the eighth layer could not break their minds as long as they had each other.

The heavy silence of the Screaming Wastes settled over the team once more, broken only by their ragged breathing. Marche kept his arm wrapped securely around Anna's waist, while Leo kept Teitra tucked safely against his side. They had survived their first true test in the abyss.

But Layer was never content to let them rest.

A sudden, sharp crackling sound—like shattering glass—echoed through the massive cavern.

The rusted floorboards beneath their boots began to violently vibrate. The deep trenches of black sludge stopped flowing, freezing completely in place.

All around them, the dead, twisted circuitry woven into the metallic bones of the wasteland surged to life. It didn't glow with the vibrant cyan of the Leviathan or the elemental colors of the crystal heart. Instead, every wire, cable, and rusted conduit ignited with a sickly, corrupted, pulsating purple light.

The illumination crawled up the towering spires like a digital infection, bathing the graveyard in a terrifying, bruised hue.

From the pooling sludge, clouds of black, corrupted particle dust began to rise. It swirled and coalesced in the air directly in front of the team, compressing rapidly. It formed a towering, formless shadow that completely blotted out the ambient light of the cavern.

Within the absolute darkness of the shadow's mass, dozens of burning, jagged purple eyes snapped open, glaring down at the four explorers with an ancient, unfathomable hatred.

"A beautiful display," a voice resonated.

It didn't echo through the cavern; it bypassed their ears entirely, vibrating directly against their skulls. The voice was a horrifying chorus of grinding metal and weeping ghosts, overlapping in a chaotic, digital harmony that made their teeth ache.

"Such fragile little threads you weave between your hearts. You call it love. You call it strength."

Marche pushed Anna slightly behind him, gripping his Nighwulf sword with both hands. The blade flared with blue lightning, but the oppressive, god-like weight of the shadow's presence made the electricity sputter and dim.

"Show yourself!" Marche yelled into the dark, refusing to yield an inch of ground.

The thousand-eyed shadow shifted, drifting closer. Its gaze bypassed the Explorer, the Watcher, and the Medic. All of its burning, jagged eyes locked exclusively onto Teitra.

"You think you have found your purpose, little Orator," the entity mocked, its voice dripping with an ancient malice that chilled the blood in their veins. "You think you are the bridge that connects these fractured souls. But a bridge is merely a structure waiting to collapse under the weight of the abyss."

Teitra swallowed hard, her golden eyes wide, but she didn't step back. She squeezed Leo's hand tightly, anchoring herself to the earth. "You're the shadow from the nightmare," she said, her voice trembling but defiant. "You're the rot the Warden warned us about."

"I am the architect of this beautiful silence," the shadow replied, the glowing circuitry around them pulsing rapidly in time with its horrific words. "Your predecessors—the Hero and his Sky Princess—they tried to understand me, too. They thought their bond could cleanse this circuitry. Do you know where they are now? They are the ghosts you hear screaming in the metal beneath your feet."

Anna gasped, her grip tightening painfully on her boltgun. "Paldyne and Melmori... they're the ones trapped in the machines?"

A deep, vibrating laugh rattled their bones.

"Their bodies failed, but I did not let their minds die. I wove them into the very foundation of this layer. They are battery and broadcast. And now, I shall do the exact same to your little party."

The ground violently lurched.

The rusted floor plates between Marche and Anna on the left, and Leo and Teitra on the right, suddenly groaned in agonizing protest. With the shriek of tearing steel, the floor snapped apart.

A massive, bottomless chasm opened up directly in the center of their formation, separating the four friends in an instant. Marche lunged forward to grab Leo's hand, but the gap was already too wide.

"Let us see how strong your precious connections truly are," the shadow hissed. It began to dissolve back into a cloud of swirling, black particles as the cavern walls began to shift, grind, and rearrange themselves like a horrific, metallic puzzle box. "Let us see if the Orator can still speak when she is dying alone in the dark."

The sickly purple light extinguished instantly. The floor beneath them tilted sharply, throwing them off their feet. Screaming each other's names, Marche, Anna, Leo, and Teitra were plunged into the grinding, shifting, pitch-black maze of the eighth layer.

CHAPTER 10
The Golden Tether

The abyssal server room was a labyrinth of rust, corrupted steel, and boiling sludge, but to Marche, Anna, and Leo, the darkness was no longer a maze. It was a straight line.

Guided by the brilliant, golden warmth of Teitra's mental connection humming in the back of their minds, the trio moved with a terrifying, synchronized efficiency. They didn't speak. They didn't need to. The Orator's psychic bridge kept their thoughts perfectly aligned, transforming three exceptional fighters into a single, unstoppable apex predator.

When a screeching pack of Crawler Husks dropped from the fleshy, diseased ceiling, Anna didn't even have to call out the targets. Through their shared mental tether, Marche already knew exactly where they were landing. Before the monsters could touch the rusted floorboards, Marche pivoted, his Nighwulf sword humming with chaotic voltage. He swung in a devastating upward arc, launching a wave of pure, blue lightning that intercepted the chimeras mid-air, reducing them to showering sparks and ash.

When the narrow aisle opened into a wider, sludge-flooded processing chamber completely guarded by towering, heavily armored Goliath Husks, Leo took the vanguard. He didn't throw his *Fire Bomb* blindly. He waited for Anna to unleash her *Flood*, sending a pressurized wave of water crashing into the beasts. The moment the water seeped into the corrupted, exposed gears of their heavy armor, Leo struck. He drove the bladed end of his cane into the ground, channeling super-heated fire directly through the wet floorboards. The water inside the chimeras' armor instantly flash-boiled into expanding steam, violently blowing the iron plating outward from the inside and exposing their purple, corrupted cores for Marche to sever.

They tore through the horrific anatomy of the eighth layer, leaving a trail of shattered metal and cleansed circuitry in their wake.

"She's close," Anna breathed, her red eyes narrowed as she sprinted over the sparking remains of a server tower. The golden warmth in her mind was growing overwhelmingly strong, vibrating with a fierce, desperate urgency. "Just past this next bulkhead!"

Miles away from the battle, suspended over a bottomless chasm of swirling, pitch-black miasma, Teitra was fighting a war of her own.

She knelt on the thick, fleshy web of bioluminescent cables, her body trembling so violently she could barely keep her head up. A thin line of blood trickled from her nose, tracking through the dirt on her pale chin. The physical toll of projecting her *Mind Melt* across the entire layer, maintaining a psychological shield for three other people while simultaneously guiding them, was pushing her brain to its absolute breaking point.

But she refused to let the golden light radiating from her skin dim.

The thousand-eyed shadow swirling in the dark abyss above her was furious. Its attempts to weave her into the corrupted circuitry were being actively repelled by the sheer purity of her emotional power.

"You are burning yourself out from the inside, little Orator," the shadow hissed, its digital, grinding voice reverberating through the cables beneath her hands, trying to shake her focus. "You cannot hold this connection forever. The human mind is a fragile vessel. It will crack. It will shatter. And when it does, the rot will consume everything you love."

"They... are coming," Teitra gritted out through clenched teeth, her golden eyes blazing as she looked up into the swirling vortex of jagged purple eyes. "And they are going to tear you apart."

The shadow let out a deafening, metallic screech of pure malice. Realizing it could not break her mind, it resorted to breaking her body.

The thick, fleshy cables beneath Teitra suddenly lost their slack. They snapped entirely taut, whipping around her wrists and ankles like living, metallic serpents.

Teitra cried out in pain as the cords constricted, lifting her spread-eagled into the air above the web. The cables pulsed with a sickly, infectious purple light, actively attempting to inject the layer's psychic agony directly into her bloodstream to force her to drop the shield.

The cold, metallic rot began to creep up her arms, numbing her fingers. Her golden aura flickered, threatening to completely collapse.

Just a little longer, Teitra prayed, squeezing her eyes shut, fighting the agonizing cold. *Please, Leo. Hurry.*

With a thunderous, explosive crash, the heavy metal bulkhead at the edge of the chasm was blown entirely off its hinges.

The heavy steel door flew through the air, tumbling into the bottomless pit. Standing in the smoking doorway, silhouetted by the blue lightning crackling off his sword, was Marche. Anna stood to his right, her boltgun raised, and Leo stood to his left, a roaring orb of fire already burning in his palm.

"Teitra!" Leo screamed, his yellow eyes widening in absolute horror as he saw her suspended in the center of the massive cavern, bound by the pulsing, corrupted cables.

"Let her go!" Marche roared, stepping out onto the edge of the chasm.

The thousand-eyed shadow materialized directly above Teitra, swirling into a massive, formless avatar of black particles and jagged purple eyes.

"You are too late, Explorers," the shadow mocked, the sound echoing like a thousand grinding gears. "She is already woven into the machine. If you sever the cables, she falls into the abyss. If you strike at me, you strike at her."

The entity was right. Teitra was suspended directly over the pitch-black void. If they destroyed the web holding her, there was nothing to stop her from plummeting into the dark sludge miles below.

But the shadow had severely underestimated the tactical brilliance of a team fighting as one.

"Anna! The chasm!" Leo ordered, his scientific mind calculating the environmental physics in a fraction of a second. "Marche, the left tethers! I've got the right!"

Anna didn't hesitate. She ran to the very edge of the precipice, holstering her boltgun and dropping to her knees. She threw both of her hands forward, pushing her *Flood* ability to its absolute maximum. She didn't summon water; she manipulated the freezing, miasmic air plunging up from the abyss. She pulled every ounce of moisture from the thick fog, condensing it rapidly directly beneath Teitra.

With a localized drop in atmospheric pressure, Anna froze the moisture into a massive, solid platform of thick, opaque ice, securely bridging the gap over the bottomless pit just ten feet below the suspended Orator.

"The floor is set! Cut her down!" Anna yelled, her arms trembling from the massive exertion.

Marche launched himself off the bulkhead, landing heavily on the newly formed ice bridge. He sprinted across the frozen platform, his Nighwulf sword trailing brilliant blue light. He leaped into the air, aiming not for the shadow, but for the thick bundle of cables tethering Teitra's left side to the ceiling.

With a deafening crack of thunder, the electrified blade sheared completely through the corrupted metal and flesh.

At the exact same moment, Leo stepped onto the ice. He spun his cane, launching a hyper-concentrated, incredibly thin *Fire Bomb*—not an explosion, but a localized, super-heated laser of pure flame. The fiery beam sliced cleanly through the cables holding Teitra's right side, melting the metal instantly without singeing a single strand of her red hair.

Severed from the ceiling, the entire web collapsed. Teitra plummeted downward.

Leo dropped his cane, lunging forward across the slippery ice. He caught her perfectly in his arms just as she hit the frozen platform, sliding backward from the momentum, absorbing the impact to keep her safe.

"I've got you," Leo breathed, holding her tightly against his chest, frantically checking her face. "Teitra, I've got you."

Teitra let out a weak, exhausted sob, burying her face in his neck, the golden light finally fading from her skin as she released her mental shield. "You made it."

"Of course we did," Leo whispered fiercely, pressing a kiss to her temple.

Above them, the thousand-eyed shadow let out a shriek of unadulterated, universe-shattering rage. The loss of its captive and the defiance of the Explorers caused the cavern to violently shake. The black particles expanded, morphing into a colossal, terrifying monstrosity of shifting metal, sludge, and blazing purple eyes, preparing to crush the ice bridge and everyone on it.

"YOU CANNOT SEVER THE ROT!" the entity roared, the psychic static hitting them like a physical gale. "I AM THE FOUNDATION OF THIS WORLD!"

Marche stood firmly at the center of the ice bridge, his Nighwulf sword raised. Anna pushed herself up, drawing her boltgun, while Leo gently set Teitra down and retrieved his bladed cane, stepping up to flank the Explorer.

Teitra refused to stay down. Ignoring the exhaustion burning in her veins, she forced herself to stand, pulling her Nighwulf sword from its sheath and joining her team on the front line.

"You aren't the foundation," Marche yelled up at the looming god of rot, his voice echoing with absolute, unbreakable conviction. He reached out, his left hand finding Anna's.

Leo reached out, his hand finding Teitra's.

"You're just a disease," Anna snarled, aiming her weapon at the densest cluster of purple eyes.

"And we are the cure," Leo added, his yellow eyes blazing as a massive, roaring inferno ignited around the blade of his cane.

Teitra closed her eyes one final time. She didn't build a shield. She weaponized her connection. She took the absolute, unyielding love, trust, and fury of her three friends, amplifying it through her *Mind Melt*, and projected it forward.

The mental attack hit the shadow first, acting as a psychic battering ram that completely shattered the entity's corrupted frequency, leaving its core entirely exposed.

"Now!" Teitra screamed.

Marche channeled every ounce of his chaotic lightning into his blade. Anna unleashed a highly pressurized, swirling vortex of water. Leo hurled a massive, blinding sphere of pure, white-hot fire.

The three elemental attacks collided perfectly in mid-air, fusing together into a devastating, localized cataclysm of boiling steam, electrocuted water, and explosive concussive force.

The combined blast struck the center of the thousand-eyed shadow.

The entity didn't even have time to scream. The sheer, overwhelming power of the Sky Kingdom's descendants completely overloaded the corrupted particles. The shadow expanded violently, its purple eyes flashing with blinding intensity before the entire mass detonated, vaporizing instantly into a harmless cloud of fine, gray ash.

The shockwave of the explosion cleared the air entirely, blowing the miasmic fog away and shattering the rusted spires hanging from the ceiling.

Silence, pure and uncorrupted, finally fell over the eighth layer.

The low-frequency, agonizing hum of the dying machines sputtered, whined, and slowly powered down completely. The sickly purple lights woven into the circuitry flickered and died. For the first time in centuries, the Screaming Wastes were entirely quiet.

The ghosts had finally been laid to rest.

On the ice bridge, the team lowered their weapons, their chests heaving, their bodies battered, bruised, and covered in soot.

Marche looked at Anna. She looked back at him, her red eyes shining with unshed tears of profound relief. He dropped his sword and pulled her into a fierce, desperate embrace, burying his face in her blonde hair.

Leo turned to Teitra. He didn't hesitate. He framed her face with his hands and kissed her deeply, pouring every ounce of his terror and his love into the absolute reality that she was alive, and she was in his arms.

When they finally pulled apart, Marche looked around the cavern. Without the fog and the corrupted shadow, the true scale of the chasm was revealed.

Anna's ice bridge connected the bulkhead they had entered from to a massive, circular stone platform on the far side of the pit.

And standing at the very back of that stone platform was the Ninth Gate.

It wasn't made of rusted metal or bleeding obsidian. It was a pristine, towering archway of polished white marble. The runes etched into its surface glowed with a soft, inviting, and incredibly pure golden light—the exact same color as Teitra's aura.

It was utterly untouched by the rot of the wasteland.

"Look at that," Marche breathed, stepping forward, his voice filled with a quiet, reverent awe.

"The corruption couldn't touch it," Leo noted, his scientific curiosity finally returning, untainted by fear. "The shadow was guarding it, keeping whatever lies beyond trapped below."

Teitra wiped the dried blood from her chin, a soft, beautiful smile touching her lips as she looked at the golden runes. "It feels... safe. It feels like the end."

Marche reached down, picking up his Nighwulf sword and sheathing it across his back. He offered his hand to Anna, his blue eyes perfectly clear.

"The Leviathan said we had to find the core," Marche said, his voice a steady, comforting anchor. "If we've cleansed the rot here, then whatever is behind those doors is the true heart of Layer."

Anna took his hand tightly. "Then let's go finish this. And let's go home."

Hand in hand, hearts steady, and their bond absolutely unbreakable, the four descendants of the Sky crossed the ice bridge. They stepped up to the pristine white marble, ready to face the final truth waiting for them in the absolute depths of the world.

CHAPTER 11
The Architect of Silence

Hand in hand, the four descendants of the Sky Kingdom crossed the threshold of the pristine, white marble archway, leaving the shattered, smoking ruins of the Screaming Wastes behind them.

The moment they stepped through, the heavy marble doors silently glided shut, instantly sealing away the suffocating stench of decay and the lingering cold of the abyss.

They found themselves standing in absolute, breathtaking tranquility.

It was a vast, spherical chamber forged entirely from flawless, polished black glass. There was no rusted metal, no boiling black sludge, and no sickening purple light. The air here was cool, crisp, and incredibly pure, smelling faintly of charged ozone and ancient, untouched stone. Woven seamlessly into the obsidian floors and sweeping curved walls were intricate lines of vibrant cyan circuitry. The glowing pathways pulsed with a calm, steady rhythm, resembling the slow, peaceful heartbeat of a sleeping giant.

It was a sanctuary. A perfect, uncorrupted quarantine zone completely untouched by the horrors outside.

Anna let out a long, shuddering exhale, the heavy boltgun finally lowering from her shoulder. Her legs, pushed to the absolute limit by the frantic acrobatics of her *Flood* ability, gave out. She dropped to her knees on the smooth glass floor, her chest heaving as the adrenaline finally began to recede.

Marche immediately knelt beside her, his Nighwulf sword clattering harmlessly against the obsidian. He wrapped his arms around her, burying his face in her neck, breathing in the scent of her hair.

A few feet away, Leo and Teitra sank to the floor together. Leo kept his arms wrapped securely around the Orator, holding her as if he was terrified the dark might reach through the marble doors and try to snatch her away again. Teitra rested her head over his heart, her golden eyes fluttering shut as she listened to the steady, comforting rhythm of his pulse.

For several long minutes, the only sound in the vast chamber was their ragged breathing. They were battered, scorched, and entirely exhausted, but looking around the circle at each other's dirt-streaked faces, a profound, overwhelming warmth filled their chests.

They were whole. The dark had thrown everything it had at them, trying to prove that their bonds were just fragile threads waiting to snap. Instead, the pressure of the abyss had forged them into unbreakable steel.

"We did it," Leo whispered, his yellow eyes shining with unshed tears. "We actually survived."

"We survived because of you," Teitra murmured, opening her eyes to look at him, then over to Marche and Anna. "Because of all of you. You didn't let me fall."

Marche offered a tired, deeply genuine smile. "We go down together. That was the promise."

As the words left his lips, the ambient hum of the chamber subtly shifted.

"Wait," Anna warned, her Watcher's instincts flaring. She gently pulled back from Marche, her red eyes darting across the smooth, reflective walls. "Do you feel that?"

The cyan circuitry beneath them suddenly surged with a brilliant, vibrating energy. The light swirled and coalesced in the dead center of the room, rising into the air like a vortex of glowing, bioluminescent dust.

The team instantly scrambled to their feet, weapons raised and elements primed. But as the particles rapidly condensed, they didn't form a jagged, terrifying chimera.

It formed a tall, imposing figure—a holographic projection of a being clad in sleek, futuristic armor that heavily resembled the divine carapace of the Leviathan they had met in the ocean above. The entity had no face; its head was a smooth, opaque glass dome that perfectly reflected Marche, Anna, Leo, and Teitra standing shoulder-to-shoulder.

Marche tensed, stepping slightly in front of the others, the blue lightning of his *Bolt Blade* crackling to life. But the entity made no aggressive moves. It simply tilted its domed head, observing them with a quiet, ancient, and profoundly sorrowful curiosity.

"You carry the fire of the surface," the entity spoke.

Its voice was not a digital, agonizing grind like the Thousand-Eyed Shadow. It was a beautiful, melodic, dual-toned chime that resonated peacefully within the glass chamber, vibrating through their bones like a tuning fork.

"And the Orator remains whole," the projection continued, its faceless gaze lingering on Teitra. "It has been an age since the Children of the Sky walked the descent."

"Who are you?" Marche demanded, his tone guarded, keeping his sword angled but ready. "Are you a guardian of the rot?"

"I am the Echo of the First Architects," the projection replied, raising a glowing, cyan hand to gesture slowly around the pristine room. "We are the ones who built the cage. We are the ones who failed."

Leo stepped out from behind Marche, his scientific curiosity completely overriding his lingering exhaustion. "The cage? You mean Layer? You built this entire subterranean ecosystem?"

The Echo turned its domed head toward the Medic.

"We did not build the abyss, brilliant one. We only built the walls to contain it." The Echo lowered its hand, its melodic voice growing heavy with the weight of millennia. "Long before the city of Orowait laid its first stones on the surface, the sky wept. A fiery tear—a glowing orange rock—streaked through the heavens and struck the heart of the ocean."

Anna and Marche exchanged a stunned, wide-eyed look. The legend of the fiery comet was a bedrock myth of Orowait. It was a story told to children before bed, the fable of the island's violent creation.

"The rock did not sleep," the Echo revealed, the cyan light in the room dimming slightly to match the somber tone. "It sank. It burrowed deep into the earth's crust, bleeding a cosmic sickness that twisted the natural life into monsters and warped metal into agony. The purple rot you fought in the wastes is not a native shadow. It is the infection of the star."

The projection pointed a glowing finger toward a massive, seamlessly integrated console at the far end of the room, overlooking a sheer drop of black glass.

"We built the descending rings to study it. Then, we built them to fight it. Finally, when the sickness proved too strong, we built these gates to quarantine it," the Echo explained. "But the star is infinitely patient. And it consumes memories. It swallowed your Hero, Paldyne, and your Princess, Melmori. It consumed their light, turning their love and their agonizing sacrifice into the very static that feeds the dark."

Anna gasped, her hand flying to her mouth. The confirmation that the founders of their bloodline—the legendary Hero and the celestial

Princess—had been tortured and consumed to power the horrific layer they had just traversed hit her like a physical blow.

Teitra's golden eyes hardened with a fierce, righteous anger. "It tried to take us, too," she said, her voice ringing with the unyielding iron of an Orator who had looked into the abyss and refused to blink. "It tried to use their memories to break us. But we aren't going to let it."

The Echo lowered its hand, looking at the four of them with a profound, quiet reverence.

"The Orator is a bridge of pure will. She touched the infection and remained whole. You all did," the Echo noted. "But hear my warning, surface dwellers: to unseal the floor of this chamber is to sever the very last pristine quarantine line of this sector. When you open the true path, the shadow will know exactly where you are. The deepest depths are no longer a cage. They are a throne room."

"We don't care," Marche stated, his voice completely devoid of hesitation. He walked directly up to the Echo and the glowing terminal. "We came down here to end this. Tell us how to open the path."

The Echo stared at Marche for a long moment. The cyan light reflected the fierce, unwavering, celestial blue of the Explorer's eyes. Slowly, the ancient, holographic projection bowed its head in a gesture of profound respect.

"Place your hands upon the runes," the Echo instructed. Its form began to slowly fade, the energy transferring from its avatar directly into the massive console. "Pour your elemental fire into the glass. Let the star know that the Children of the Sky still burn."

The Echo dissolved entirely into glowing dust, leaving the team alone in the silent room.

Leo, Anna, and Teitra immediately rushed to Marche's side. They didn't need to discuss it. They surrounded the crystalline terminal, placing their hands over the glowing, pulsing cyan runes carved into the black glass.

"Ready?" Marche asked, his voice steady over the deep, resonant hum of the chamber.

"Open the door," Anna whispered fiercely.

"Let's bring them peace," Teitra added, her golden eyes focused.

"Let's finish the diagnosis," Leo finalized, his yellow eyes locked onto the console.

Without another word, the four Explorers unleashed their ancient, ancestral fire.

Marche channeled the chaotic, roaring energy of his *Bolt Blade* directly through his palms, sending a surge of blinding blue lightning into the glass. Beside him, Anna called upon her *Flood*, her hands glowing with a deep, pressurized azure light that carried the crushing weight of the ocean. Leo pushed his *Fire Bomb* to its absolute limit, the white-hot heat of plasma radiating from his fingertips. And Teitra expanded her *Mind Melt*, pouring a brilliant, pure golden aura of love and unbreakable connection into the machinery.

The crystalline terminal drank it all in.

The pristine, cyan circuitry of the room didn't just accept their power; it perfectly synchronized with it. The runes flared violently, swirling with blue, azure, white, and gold light. The polished black glass of the room vibrated, resonating with the sheer, uncorrupted emotional and elemental force of the team's bond.

A deafening, pneumatic *CRACK* echoed through the chamber, sounding like a planetary fault line snapping.

The floor of the obsidian room trembled violently. Through the massive, sweeping glass window at the edge of the chamber, the pitch-black abyss beyond began to violently shift.

The swirling, toxic smog that had hidden the true bottom of the eighth layer was forcefully sucked downward, clearing the air.

Slowly, agonizingly, an impossibly massive structure began to rise from the dark miles below. It wasn't a rusted gate, and it wasn't a stone archway. It was a colossal, jagged tear in the very fabric of the earth itself.

It was a bleeding, cosmic wound in the bedrock, radiating a sickly, pulsating, blinding orange light—the exact color of the comet from the legends.

The infection of the star had been fully unquarantined.

The path to the Ninth Gate, the throne room of the rot, was finally open.

Marche slowly pulled his hands back from the terminal, the blue lightning fading from his fingertips. His bright eyes reflected the ominous, towering orange glow filling the massive viewing window.

He reached over his shoulder, gripping the hilt of his Nighwulf sword. The chimera-bone blade slid from its sheath with a lethal *shing*, feeling lighter, sharper, and deadlier in his hands than ever before.

"The Echo said the star consumes memories," Marche said, his voice as hard and uncompromising as iron.

He turned around, looking at his three best friends. He looked at the family he had bled for, and the family he was completely ready to die for.

"Let's go make sure it remembers us."

Chapter 12
The Heart of the Crater

The opalescent dome had been their final sanctuary, a fleeting breath of peace in a world designed to crush them. As Marche, Anna, Leo, and Teitra stepped out from the frosted glass archway and back into the sprawling, ashen wasteland, the Ninth Layer welcomed them with a violent, atmospheric roar.

Thrum.

The heartbeat of the star pounded through the bedrock, so unimaginably loud that it vibrated in the marrow of their bones. The crystalline ash, which had previously fallen like a gentle winter flurry, was now a chaotic, blinding blizzard. With every massive exhale of the cosmic entity, the white dust was blasted outward like a shockwave. With every inhale, the freezing vacuum dragged the ash violently back toward the center of the cavern.

Marche leaned forward into the gale, his modified Nighwulf sword drawn. The cyan ash he had meticulously rubbed into the leather hilt flared to life, resonating with his pulse. The *Bolt Blade* didn't just crackle; it hummed with a concentrated, localized static field that anchored him to the ground.

"Stay close!" Marche roared over the howling wind, his voice barely audible. "Follow the light!"

Anna walked directly behind him, her Watcher's eyes narrowed against the stinging glass-dust. She held her boltgun tight against her chest, the modified rounds securely loaded. Leo and Teitra flanked her, their heads bowed against the tempest, their hands firmly locked together.

They trudged through the petrified museum of the First Architects. The flawless, transparent glass statues of ancient chimeras cast long, distorted shadows in the sickly, pulsating orange light that bled from the horizon. But as they marched closer to the epicenter, the statues began to change.

They weren't just frozen monuments anymore. With every tectonic heartbeat of the star, a faint, liquid orange fire flickered deep within the transparent, glass chests of the beasts.

"Leo!" Teitra shouted, her golden eyes widening as the wavy purple haze of her *Mind Melt* flared defensively to life. "The statues! They aren't dead!"

"They're conductors!" Leo realized, his clinical mind piecing the nightmare together as he raised his bladed cane. "The star is using the ambient energy to reanimate them!"

As if responding to his words, the cavern let out a deafening, harmonic shatter.

All around them, the glass chimeras violently jerked. The liquid orange fire within their transparent veins flared into blinding brilliance. The statues tore their vitrified limbs from the deep ash, the sound of grinding, screeching glass echoing like a thousand fingernails on a chalkboard.

A massive, four-armed glass behemoth directly in their path unhinged its razor-sharp mandibles and let out a roar that sounded like shattering windows.

"Break them!" Marche commanded.

The behemoth charged, its heavy glass hooves churning the ash. Marche didn't step back. He lunged forward, swinging his Nighwulf sword in a devastating, two-handed arc. The chimera-bone blade struck the beast's transparent foreleg.

The cyan ash woven into Marche's hilt worked exactly as he had engineered. The blue lightning of his *Bolt Blade* didn't just strike and dissipate; it latched onto the glass. The localized static charge violently paralyzed the creature's crystalline joints. The behemoth seized, suspended mid-stride, its internal orange fire violently clashing with the blue voltage. With a sharp twist of his blade, Marche shattered the beast's paralyzed leg, sending the colossal monster crashing into the dunes where it splintered into a million harmless, glowing shards.

But there were hundreds more waking up.

A pack of sleek, glass hounds bounded over the dunes, their transparent jaws snapping wildly.

"I've got the flank!" Anna yelled. She dropped to one knee, leveled her boltgun, and pulled the trigger.

The heavy bolt tore through the gale and struck the lead hound square in the chest. The moment the round impacted, the cyan ash packed inside the casing reacted with Anna's *Flood* ability. Instead of a splash of water, a highly pressurized, localized explosion of absolute zero ice erupted inside the creature. The rapid freeze violently expanded within the hound's enclosed glass body, shattering it from the inside out in a spectacular burst of frozen shrapnel.

Anna racked the bolt, a fierce, triumphant smirk crossing her face. "The modifications work! Keep them contained!"

Leo spun his cane, stepping back-to-back with Teitra. The glass horde was swarming from the right. He didn't bother with small, precise strikes. He dug deep into the ancient magic in his veins, his yellow eyes burning like twin suns.

"Get behind my shield!" Teitra called out, projecting a massive, telekinetic dome of pure golden energy over the team, deflecting the razor-sharp shards of glass raining down from Anna and Marche's kills.

Leo thrust his free hand forward, unleashing a massive, roaring *Fire Bomb*. But he didn't aim at the chimeras; he aimed directly at the ash beneath their feet.

The white-hot plasma hit the crystalline dunes with the force of a meteor. The sheer, unadulterated heat of his fire instantly super-heated the glass-dust, melting the entire dune into a sprawling pool of bubbling, molten slag. The charging glass chimeras ran directly into the super-heated trap, their legs melting and fusing to the floor, trapping them helplessly in the magma before Anna methodically shattered them from afar.

They fought like gods of the old world. Teitra's mental bridge kept their movements utterly flawless. They danced through the shattering horde, a perfectly synchronized hurricane of ice, lightning, and fire, carving a path of destruction straight toward the center of the world.

Thrum.

The heartbeat hit again, so violently it knocked them all off balance. The remaining glass chimeras didn't attack; they suddenly froze, their orange inner fires dimming as they turned and bowed their transparent heads toward the horizon.

The ash storm abruptly died. The vacuum ceased.

The team scrambled to their feet, their weapons raised, breathing heavily in the sudden, terrifying silence.

They had reached the edge of the crater.

The ground dropped away into a massive, bowl-shaped depression in the bedrock, easily a mile across. At the very bottom of the crater, hovering just inches above a pool of boiling, corrupted black sludge, was the star.

It was a cosmic parasite of incomprehensible scale. It wasn't a perfect sphere; it was a jagged, visceral mass of molten orange rock and pulsing, fleshy purple veins. It looked exactly like a massive, diseased, anatomically correct heart torn from the chest of a titan.

Thick, glowing tendrils of the star's infection dug deep into the bedrock of the crater, pumping its sickness upward into the eight layers above. It was the absolute core of the rot. It was the architect of the silence.

And hovering directly in front of the colossal, beating star were two figures.

Marche's blood ran completely cold. The Nighwulf sword trembled in his hands.

They were human-sized, suspended in the air by thick, pulsing tethers of orange light connected to the star's core.

One figure was a towering man clad in a heavy, archaic crimson cape and dark, earthen armor. His broadsword hung limply at his side. The other figure was a woman in a flowing, tattered white dress, her hair as pale as moonlight, gently floating in the zero-gravity field of the star.

Their bodies were perfectly preserved, but their eyes were closed, their faces etched with centuries of unending, silent agony.

"No..." Anna gasped, her boltgun lowering slightly as the sheer, heartbreaking horror of the sight washed over her.

"Paldyne and Melmori," Leo whispered, his voice cracking.

The star had not just consumed their memories. It had kept their physical bodies as the ultimate, eternal batteries for its quarantine-breaking rot.

Suddenly, the star pulsed with a blinding, aggressive flare of orange light.

Teitra screamed, falling to her knees on the edge of the crater. Her hands flew to her temples, her golden eyes widening in absolute, universe-shattering terror as the star bypassed her psychic shields completely.

"I HAVE TASTED THE HEAVENS, AND I HAVE DEVOURED THE EARTH," a voice—a thousand overlapping voices of pure,

cosmic hunger—echoed not just in their minds, but vibrating through the very fabric of reality.

The eyes of the suspended figures—the first Hero and the Sky Princess—violently snapped open. But they weren't human eyes. They burned with the same sickly, pulsating orange light as the star behind them.

The star was using their ancestors as its final avatars.

"AND NOW, CHILDREN," the star's voice ground against their skulls, *"I WILL DEVOUR YOUR FUTURE."*

The possessed avatar of Paldyne raised his ancient broadsword, the blade instantly igniting with a corrupted, orange copy of Marche's own lightning. The avatar of Melmori raised her pale hands, summoning a swirling, dark vortex of boiling sludge and crushed gravity.

"Teitra! Block it out!" Leo yelled, dropping to his knees to shield her as the psychic weight of the star tried to crush her mind.

"I can't!" Teitra sobbed, blood beginning to trickle from her nose. "It's too massive! It's pulling their memories... it's showing me what it did to them!"

Marche stepped up to the very edge of the precipice. The awe and the horror completely vanished from his face, replaced by a cold, calculating, and absolutely lethal fury. He looked at the tortured, puppet-like forms of the legends who had founded his city. He looked at the star that had kept them trapped in hell for centuries.

"Anna," Marche said, his voice dropping to a terrifying, absolute calm.

Anna stepped up beside him, racking the final, cyan-loaded bolt into the chamber of her weapon. Her red eyes burned with a righteous, uncompromising vengeance. "I'm with you."

"Leo. Teitra. Get up," Marche ordered, not looking back. "We don't bow to the past. We break it."

Teitra wiped the blood from her chin, forcing herself to her feet with Leo's help. She drew her Nighwulf sword, pushing the agony of the star to the back of her mind, channeling every ounce of her remaining strength into the golden bridge connecting her team.

The possessed avatars of the Hero and the Princess launched themselves upward from the bottom of the crater, flying toward them with god-like speed, trailing cosmic fire and dark magic.

"For Orowait," Marche roared, raising his crackling blade to the sky.

"For Orowait!" the team screamed in perfect unison.

With absolute, unbreakable devotion, the four Explorers threw themselves over the edge of the crater, plunging downward to clash with the legends of the past and deliver the final, killing blow to the heart of the world.

CHAPTER 13
The Glass Crucible

Stepping out of the pearlescent dome felt like leaving the only warm room in a dead, frozen castle.

The crystalline ash immediately began to cling to their boots again, sparkling like crushed diamonds in the dim, sickly orange light that bled from the unseen center of the cavern. Marche took the lead, his Nighwulf sword drawn. The newly rubbed cyan ash in the hilt pulsed with a faint, contained energy, humming against his palm, waiting to be unleashed.

Anna flanked him to the right, her boltgun raised and loaded with the experimental, cyan-laced shatter rounds. Leo and Teitra followed closely behind, their eyes darting between the towering, flash-frozen glass chimeras that littered the dunes.

And beneath it all was the rhythm.

Thrum. The bass note vibrated through the bedrock, rattling the iron in their blood.

Inhale. The air pressure in the massive cavern dropped, creating a sudden, freezing vacuum that pulled the white ash, and their heavy cloaks, violently forward toward the crater's center.

Exhale. A rush of superheated, toxic wind blasted back against them, carrying the suffocating stench of burning ozone and ancient decay.

They used the heavy breathing of the star as a twisted metronome. When the comet inhaled, they marched forward, letting the draft assist their descent down the massive, sloping dunes. When it exhaled, they crouched low behind the colossal glass statues, using the petrified horrors as windbreaks against the searing heat.

"The statues are getting denser," Anna called out over the rushing wind, her red eyes squinting against the blowing ash. She swept the barrel of her boltgun across a cluster of frozen, multi-limbed predators that looked as though they had been sprinting away from the center when the comet's flash-freeze caught them. "It's like they were all trying to escape the blast radius."

"They were the first quarantine line," Leo theorized, his yellow eyes wide with grim realization as he looked at the sheer volume of vitrified monsters. "The star didn't just burn them. It glassed them. It turned the entire ecosystem into a physical barrier to protect itself."

"Well, the barrier is broken now," Marche grunted, pushing past the frozen, translucent coils of a towering serpent.

As they crested the final, massive dune of white ash, the ground beneath their boots abruptly changed. The soft, crunching powder completely gave way to a perfectly smooth, frictionless surface.

They had reached the edge of the inner crater.

The four Explorers stopped dead in their tracks, looking down into the massive, bowl-shaped depression. The floor of the crater wasn't rock or dirt; it was a sheer, concave slope of solid, black glass, formed by the unimaginable heat of the comet's initial impact thousands of years ago.

And resting at the very bottom of the bowl was the Astral Blight.

It was horrifying in its sheer, alien geometry. It wasn't a beast of flesh and blood, but a colossal monolith of shifting, pitch-black obsidian plates. The massive plates constantly folded and slid over one another like a colossal puzzle box, desperately trying to contain the terrifying, blinding orange light of the core burning within.

Sprawling out from the base of the monolith were massive, fleshy roots made of the exact same corrupted, purple circuitry they had fought in the eighth layer. The roots were dug deep into the black glass of the crater, glowing with a sickly pulse as they pumped the star's infection directly into the bedrock of Orowait above.

Thrum. The obsidian plates shifted open just a fraction, revealing a sliver of the dying sun inside. The heat radiating up the glass bowl was instantaneous and oppressive, instantly vaporizing a layer of sweat on their skin.

Teitra grabbed Leo's arm, her golden eyes wide with a profound, existential terror. "It's so heavy, Leo. The gravity... it's pulling on my mind. It's so hungry."

"It's not going to eat anything else today," Marche said, his voice as cold as the ice Anna commanded.

He didn't hesitate. He stepped over the lip of the crater, his boots finding a precarious grip on the sloped black glass. "Slide down. Keep your weapons ready. If it inhales while we're on the slope, drop your center of gravity immediately or it'll pull you right into the core."

Anna went next, using a tiny fraction of her *Flood* to create a thin layer of frost under her boots, giving her perfect traction on the slick glass. Leo helped Teitra down, keeping his body positioned protectively between her and the burning monolith.

They slid down the massive, concave slope together in absolute silence, the towering monolith growing larger and far more imposing with every yard. Scattered across the bottom of the glass bowl, forming a tight ring around the comet, were dozens of the largest, most terrifying flash-frozen glass chimeras they had seen yet.

As Marche's boots finally hit the flat floor of the crater's bottom, the rhythmic breathing abruptly stopped.

The wind died. The ash suspended in the air froze in place. The suffocating silence of the Ashen Sanctuary returned, but this time, it felt like a steel trap springing shut.

The colossal obsidian plates of the monolith slowly stopped shifting. Deep within the core, the blinding orange light flared. It didn't release a wave of heat; it released a massive, silent pulse of pure, concentrated astral energy.

The orange light washed over the arena, passing through Marche, Anna, Leo, and Teitra without harming them. But as the light hit the ring of towering, petrified glass chimeras surrounding them, the impossible happened.

The perfect, silent glass began to loudly, violently crack.

The sound of shattering crystal echoed like a hundred gunshots across the bowl. The frozen, translucent statues jerked. Slowly, unnaturally, the glass monsters turned their jagged, featureless heads toward the four Explorers. The orange light of the star ignited within their hollow, transparent chests, acting as a surrogate heartbeat.

"They aren't statues anymore," Anna warned, racking the bolt of her gun.

The heavy metallic *clack* signaled the end of the peace.

The Glass Vanguard let out a deafening, unified roar that sounded like grinding crystal, and charged.

They didn't move with the fleshy, decaying clumsiness of the Hollowed Husks. Animated entirely by the star's concentrated astral energy, the massive glass chimeras lunged with terrifying, weightless speed. Their jagged, translucent claws scraped against the frictionless obsidian floor, producing a sound like a thousand knives dragging across slate.

"Spread out!" Marche roared, dropping into a defensive stance. "Don't let them box us against the monolith!"

A towering, wolf-like creature forged from perfectly clear, vitrified crystal reached him first. It leapt across the smooth black glass, its jaws opening wide, the pulsing orange light of the star burning fiercely within its hollow chest.

Marche didn't dodge. He gripped his Nighwulf sword with both hands and swung a massive, upward arc.

The collision of chimera-bone against solid crystal rang out with a deafening, bell-like *CLANG*. The sheer physical force of the beast nearly knocked Marche off his feet, his boots slipping backward on the slick slope.

But as the blade bit into the beast's translucent shoulder, the newly applied cyan ash ignited.

The *Bolt Blade* didn't just discharge a flash of chaotic blue lightning. The uncorrupted cyan dust acted like an energetic glue. A web of brilliant, crackling electricity surged outward from the cut, clinging directly to the glass.

The wolf chimera let out a grinding shriek as the lingering static charge seized its crystalline anatomy. Its front legs locked entirely, the joints paralyzed by the relentless electrical current. It crashed hard onto the obsidian floor, sliding helplessly toward the team.

"Anna! The joints!" Marche yelled, staggering back to regain his balance.

Anna was already tracking the beast through her boltgun's iron sights. She pulled the trigger.

BANG.

The heavy bolt struck the paralyzed chimera directly in its electrified shoulder. The moment the casing shattered, the experimental payload deployed. A concentrated burst of water infused with the cyan ash flooded into the electrically charged cracks.

The chemical reaction was instantaneous. The water flash-froze into massive, rapidly expanding spikes of solid ice inside the beast's glass shell. Unable to contain the extreme pressure, the chimera violently detonated. Thousands of razor-sharp glass shards exploded outward, raining down onto the black slope like harmless hail.

"It works!" Anna shouted, a fierce grin breaking through the grime on her face as she racked another round. "Keep locking them down, Marche!"

"With pleasure!" Marche surged forward, his sword a blur of lingering blue static as he parried the slashing claws of a two-headed glass serpent, instantly paralyzing its coiled body for Anna to shatter.

For a fleeting moment, their newly crafted gear made them feel invincible. They moved with the flawless, mind-linked synchronization Teitra had forged in the upper layers.

But the star was not a mindless beast. It was a calculating parasite.

As Marche drove his electrified blade into the chest of a four-armed behemoth, the colossal obsidian monolith at the center of the crater pulsed.

Thrum.

The star inhaled.

The sudden, violent shift in air pressure created a massive gravity well that ripped across the frictionless floor. The draft was so incredibly powerful it physically yanked Marche forward. His boots lost their grip on the slick black glass, and he went down hard, sliding uncontrollably toward the blinding, burning heat of the core.

The glass chimeras, weightless and entirely unbothered by the lack of traction, used the gravity well to their advantage. They accelerated, riding the draft directly into the team.

"Marche!" Anna screamed, trying to plant her feet to fire, but the vacuum pulled her off balance. Her shot went wide, the shatter-round exploding uselessly against the indestructible obsidian wall of the monolith.

The four-armed behemoth Marche had just struck didn't shatter. The static charge had paralyzed its lower half, but as it slid down the slope alongside him, it swung one of its massive, jagged crystalline arms.

The razor-sharp glass sheared straight through Marche's repaired leather breastplate.

Marche let out a choked cry of agony as the crystal sliced deep into his side. Hot blood instantly spilled out, splashing stark red against the pristine, transparent arm of the monster.

"Get off him!" Leo roared.

The Medic sprinted down the slick slope, his yellow eyes blazing. He swung his Nighwulf cane like a baseball bat, aiming for the beast's head. But he miscalculated the density of the star-forged glass.

The impact snapped the beast's neck, but the sheer kinetic blow shattered the upper half of the creature entirely. A localized explosion of jagged shrapnel erupted directly in Leo's face.

Leo threw his arms up, but a massive shard of glass drove itself deep into his left shoulder, pinning his arm to his side. The force of the shrapnel threw him backward, his head cracking sickeningly against the solid obsidian floor.

"Leo!" Teitra shrieked. The golden light of her *Mind Melt* flared violently as she watched the Medic hit the ground, his green coat rapidly soaking with dark blood.

The gravity well finally snapped shut. The air pressure equalized with a deafening *Exhale*, blasting a shockwave of superheated wind across the bowl that sent the remaining glass chimeras skidding backward.

Marche groaned, clutching his bleeding side. He dug the tip of his electrified sword into a seam in the black glass to arrest his slide, stopping just twenty yards from the burning, fleshy purple roots of the monolith.

Anna scrambled down the slope, her hands coated in frost to keep her balance, throwing herself fiercely between Marche and the regrouping monsters.

Teitra dropped to her knees beside Leo. His eyes were half-closed, his breathing shallow as his right hand weakly gripped the jagged piece of glass embedded in his opposite shoulder.

"Don't pull it out," Teitra commanded, her voice shaking violently as she pressed her hands around the wound, trying to staunch the bleeding. "Leo, stay with me. Please stay with me."

"I'm... fine," Leo wheezed, coughing weakly. He looked past her, his eyes locking onto the center of the crater. "Teitra... the core."

Teitra turned her head.

The remaining Glass Vanguard chimeras weren't charging. They were retreating, moving backward to form a protective ring around the base of the monolith.

The colossal, black obsidian plates of the Astral Blight were grinding loudly. Driven by the failure of its physical puppets to execute the intruders, the parasite decided to stop hiding behind glass.

The plates violently folded outward, slamming heavily into the crater floor.

The blinding, dying-sun orange light of the core was fully exposed. It radiated a wave of thermal energy so intense that the crystalline ash scattered across the arena instantly flash-vaporized. The heat hit the team like a physical wall, suffocating and agonizingly bright.

The heat was absolute. It wasn't the warmth of a hearth or the dry burn of a desert; it was the suffocating, unadulterated radiation of a dying star. Within seconds of the obsidian plates peeling back, the air inside the crater turned into a physical weapon.

Marche collapsed onto one knee, coughing violently as the superheated air scorched his lungs. The edges of his scorched leather armor began to smoke, the smell of burning hide mixing with the coppery tang of the blood pouring from his side.

Anna threw her arms up, instantly calling upon her *Flood* to create a shimmering dome of water vapor over them, but the moisture hissed and evaporated the moment it materialized, turning into scalding steam.

"I can't hold it back!" Anna yelled, her red eyes watering against the blinding light. "It's evaporating the moisture from the air itself!"

Teitra was curled over Leo, trying to use her own body to shield him from the blinding radiation, but her clothes were already beginning to smolder.

"We're going to cook alive," Marche grunted, trying to stand, but his boots slipped on the slick, burning glass.

The remaining Glass Vanguard didn't attack. They didn't need to. They stood in a perfect, silent ring, watching the intruders burn.

No. The thought wasn't spoken aloud. It echoed through their minds, weak and ragged, but undeniably stubborn.

Beneath Teitra, Leo moved. His left arm hung completely useless, pinned to his side by the jagged glass shrapnel, but his right hand clamped fiercely around the intricately carved wood of his Nighwulf cane.

"Leo, don't move," Teitra pleaded, tears streaming down her soot-stained face, instantly evaporating on her cheeks. "You're bleeding too much."

"Thermodynamics, Teitra," Leo rasped, forcing his yellow eyes open. He pushed past her hands, using his cane to leverage himself upright. He swayed violently, his face deathly pale beneath the dirt, but he locked his knees, staring directly into the blinding core of the Astral Blight.

Marche. Anna. Leo's voice projected through Teitra's mental bridge, crystal clear despite his physical agony. *You can't fight a star with fire. You have to starve it.*

Leo didn't spin his cane. He didn't summon a spark. Instead, he slammed the base of the wood hard against the frictionless obsidian floor and opened his consciousness to the ambient energy of the crater.

He reversed his elemental flow.

Instead of projecting heat outward to create a *Fire Bomb*, Leo turned himself into a thermal vacuum.

The oppressive, lethal radiation radiating from the exposed core was suddenly yanked violently off the team. The air around the four Explorers dropped from a blistering, lethal fever to a chilling, breathable cold in a matter of seconds.

Above Leo's cane, a swirling, localized vortex of white-hot plasma began to furiously spin, absorbing the massive influx of stellar heat. The sheer volume of energy was terrifying. The plasma burned so brightly it rivaled the core itself, but Leo held the magnetic containment field together with sheer, unyielding willpower, his teeth gritted in agony.

"Anna!" Leo screamed aloud, the veins in his neck bulging. "Now! Hit the core!"

Anna didn't hesitate. Shielded by Leo's thermal vacuum, the Watcher stepped out from behind Marche. She unslung her boltgun, dropping it to the glass floor. This wasn't a job for a firearm.

She raised both her hands, her red eyes burning with a freezing, oceanic fury. She reached deep into the reserves of her *Flood*, pulling every microscopic drop of moisture from her own body, from the sweat on Marche's brow, and from the deep, subterranean water table buried miles beneath the bedrock of Orowait.

A massive, pressurized sphere of deep azure water materialized between her palms. But she didn't just throw it. She reached into her pouch, grabbing a handful of the uncorrupted cyan ash, and crushed it directly into the sphere.

The water didn't just freeze. It dropped to absolute zero. The sphere turned into a jagged, swirling mass of hyper-dense, cyan-infused frost.

"Marche, the Vanguard!" Anna yelled, her arms trembling under the immense weight of the cold.

Seeing the massive buildup of elemental energy, the ring of glass chimeras finally broke their formation. Three towering, translucent beasts lunged across the smooth floor to intercept her.

Marche ignored the agonizing pain in his side. He roared, stepping directly in front of Anna. He swung his Nighwulf sword in a massive, horizontal arc, unleashing a blinding wave of the Lingering Static. The chaotic blue electricity crashed into the charging beasts, paralyzing their glass joints mid-leap and sending them crashing harmlessly against the slick floor.

"Clear!" Marche shouted.

Anna thrust both hands forward.

The sphere of absolute zero erupted into a massive, sustained beam of freezing, azure energy. It tore across the crater, completely bypassing the paralyzed Vanguard, and slammed directly into the exposed, boiling orange core of the Astral Blight.

The collision of extreme temperatures was catastrophic.

For a split second, the blinding orange light and the deep azure frost fought in a silent, perfectly balanced stalemate.

Then, physics took over.

The rapid, immense cooling of the superheated stellar matter caused a violent thermal shock. A deafening, world-shaking *CRACK* echoed through the massive cavern, louder than the Leviathan's roar, louder than the dying machinery of the eighth layer.

The flawless, impenetrable surface of the star's core physically fractured.

Massive, jagged fissures spider-webbed across the glowing orange surface, violently leaking thick, corrupted purple sludge. The blinding light of the comet sputtered, glitched, and instantly dimmed.

The sudden drop in astral energy severed the puppet strings. All around them, the remaining Glass Vanguard collapsed into lifeless heaps of shattered crystal.

The massive gravity well died. The blistering heat vanished, replaced by a cool, stagnant subterranean air. At the center of the crater, the colossal obsidian plates hung limp, unable to close over the broken, bleeding core of the star.

They had done it. They had physically broken the god that fell from the sky.

Leo's plasma shield dissipated with a soft hiss. The Medic dropped his cane, his eyes rolling back in his head as he collapsed backward onto the black glass. Teitra caught him, her own tears finally falling freely as she cradled his head in her lap.

Marche dropped to his knees, his sword clattering against the floor, his hand pressing desperately against the deep gash in his side. He looked up at the fractured, dimming monolith, a ragged, blood-stained grin breaking across his face.

Anna fell back onto her hands, her breath coming in heavy, exhausted gasps. She looked at Marche, then at the broken core, her chest heaving with a triumphant, disbelieving laugh.

"We broke it," Anna breathed, the echo of her voice carrying across the silent, glass crucible. "Marche, we actually broke it."

But the Astral Blight was not a machine of gears and metal. It was a parasite. And as the physical core bled its purple rot onto the floor, a new, far more insidious energy began to leak from the cracks.

The cavern didn't heat up. It didn't pull them in. Instead, the air grew unnaturally, terrifyingly heavy with the weight of stolen memories.

Marche didn't hesitate. Ignoring the agonizing tear in his side, he gripped his Nighwulf sword with both hands, the cyan ash in the hilt flaring with blinding blue lightning. Driven by Teitra's psychic hold on the star, he sprinted across the slick, black glass, leapt onto the fractured obsidian shell, and drove the electrified chimera-bone blade directly into the bleeding, orange heart of the Astral Blight.

The blade sank to the hilt.

For a terrifying, stretched second, the universe held its breath.

The dying sun inside the monolith pulsed once, a violent, blinding strobe of pure white light.

Then, the star exhaled for the final time.

There was no deafening explosion. There was no concussive shockwave of fire. Instead, a silent, absolute wave of pure, crystalline energy washed out from the severed core.

It was the original, uncorrupted quarantine protocol of the First Architects, triggered by the death of the parasite.

The wave passed through the crater instantly, vaporizing the fleshy purple roots and wiping away the suffocating psychic weight of the Memory Eater entirely.

Marche dropped from the monolith, landing heavily on the glass floor. He let out a ragged gasp, reaching for his bleeding side, but his hand stopped mid-air. The pain was gone.

"Marche..." Anna whispered.

He looked down. His heavy leather boots had lost their color, shifting into a flawless, translucent crystal. The transformation was creeping steadily up his calves, vitrifying his armor, his clothes, and his skin into perfectly clear, indestructible glass.

It didn't hurt. It felt like stepping into a freezing, numbing winter river.

Anna fell to her knees a few yards away, her boltgun slipping from her grasp and clattering against the floor. Her legs were already frozen to the black glass.

"It's the quarantine," Leo rasped, his voice barely a whisper. He was lying in Teitra's lap, his uninjured arm lifting weakly to look at his own hand. His fingers were turning transparent, catching the fading light of the cavern. "The star is dead... but the layer is sealing itself. We're the final barrier."

"No," Marche grunted, trying to force his legs to move, but they were entirely locked. The panic finally set in. "No, we made a promise! We're supposed to build a home!"

Anna dragged herself across the smooth floor, her crystallized legs dragging uselessly behind her. She reached Marche, throwing her arms around his waist. Marche dropped to his knees, wrapping his large arms tightly around her shoulders as the freezing glass crept up his thighs.

"We are," Anna sobbed, burying her face against his chest, her tears turning to tiny diamonds as they fell. "Marche, we saved it. We saved Orowait. It's over. We *are* the foundation."

A few feet away, Teitra pulled Leo tightly against her chest. The golden glow of her *Mind Melt* was fading, replaced by the soft, milky iridescence of the glass creeping up her spine. She rested her cheek against his green hair, rocking him gently.

"I've got you, Leo," Teitra whispered, a sad, beautiful smile touching her lips as her golden eyes met his. "I've got you. You don't have to carry the weight anymore."

"Teitra..." Leo breathed, a crystalline tear freezing on his cheek. "I love you."

"I know," she murmured, closing her eyes as the glass reached her heart.

Marche buried his face in Anna's red hair, holding her as tightly as he possibly could. He closed his eyes, imagining the sun warming the grass at the top of the well, imagining the wind coming off the ocean. He held onto that dream, and he held onto the woman he loved, as the final wave of silence overtook them.

The cavern fell perfectly, eternally still.

At the bottom of the black crater, surrounding the dead, ash-covered monolith, sat four flawless glass statues.

A Watcher and an Explorer, locked in a fierce, protective embrace. A Medic and an Orator, resting peacefully in each other's arms.

And as the last of the falling white ash settled over the arena, the dimming light revealed they were not alone.

Just a few paces away, standing vigil over the shattered core, were two older statues of perfect, transparent glass. A tall man resting his hands on the hilt of a greatsword, and a beautiful woman holding a celestial staff. Their glass hands were intertwined.

Paldyne and Melmori.

The original heroes had never left the quarantine zone. They had sacrificed themselves to stall the star, waiting in the silence for centuries until four children from the sky finally arrived to finish what they started.

Together, the six statues rested in the Ashen Sanctuary, guarding the deep forever.

EPILOGUE
The Legacy of Glass

Generations later, the island city of Orowait flourished brilliantly under the warm, unyielding sun. The air was filled with the sounds of bustling markets, the laughter of children, and the gentle rustle of fertile farmlands. At the absolute center of the city, the great stone doors of the First Layer were permanently sealed, locked tight against an abyss that had fallen perfectly, eternally silent.

The monsters of the deep—the Nighwulfs, the Husks, the Leviathans—were no longer immediate threats; they had faded into myth, nothing more than frightening stories told to wide-eyed children around the hearth at night.

High above the cobblestone streets, in the grand, sunlit libraries of the city, the Orators faithfully taught the history of their salvation. They stood before massive tapestries, their voices ringing with pride as they told the tale of the First Heroes: Paldyne, the weapon forged by the earth, and Melmori, the Princess of the Sky.

The archives stated as absolute, historical fact that the heroes descended into the dark, defeated the shadow, and returned to the sunlight, battered but triumphant. The official records claimed that Paldyne and Melmori lived long, peaceful lives, ruling the city with wisdom and grace, and raising their beloved daughter, Reverie, before passing away quietly in their sleep. It was a history of absolute triumph and unwavering romance.

It was also a desperate, beautiful lie.

The burden of the truth was a heavy, suffocating secret known only to the High Council of the first era. When Paldyne and Melmori descended into the well on that fateful day centuries ago, they knew with absolute certainty it was a one-way journey. They knew the cosmic star required a permanent, physical quarantine. But before they left the surface forever, they made the ultimate sacrifice, entrusting their infant daughter, Reverie, to the care of the city's elders.

When the poisonous miasma finally cleared and the island stopped shaking, the elders knew the heroes had succeeded. But they also realized the devastating truth of the sacrifice. If the citizens of Orowait learned that their greatest champions were permanently entombed in glass at the bottom of a hellish abyss, the psychological toll would completely shatter the city's spirit. The sheer, existential fear of the well would consume them, rotting Orowait from the inside out.

So, the elders made a choice. They forged a myth.

They hid Reverie's true age, claiming to the public that she was born after the heroes returned from the dark. They hired actors to wear the heavy crimson cape of Paldyne and the flowing white dress of Melmori, parading them from afar during festivals before claiming the heroes had retired to the highest, most secluded towers of the city. And when the appropriate time came, they announced the heroes' peaceful passing and held grand, weeping, but entirely empty funerals.

They deliberately rewrote history to give Orowait a legacy of hope, rather than a legacy of despair. They needed the future generations of Explorers, Watchers, Medics, and Orators to look at the sealed well and believe that the darkness could not only be beaten, but survived.

And centuries later, that fabricated, shining hope is exactly what gave a young Explorer named Marche, a fierce Watcher named Anna, a brilliant Medic named Leo, and a devoted Orator named Teitra the courage to step onto the lift and jump into the dark.

They had descended believing in a happy ending. Because of that lie, they had fought with unyielding ferocity, their minds protected by the belief that love could conquer the abyss and return to the sun.

The lie saved the world.

But miles beneath the earth, far below thc bustling markets, the grand libraries, and the warm sunlight, the truth remained perfectly preserved.

Down through the Endless Plains, past the Twisted Forest, beneath the freezing peaks and the silent oceans, the Ninth Layer rested in eternal, undisturbed peace. The white crystalline ash covered the floor of the massive crater like a blanket of fresh snow.

There, resting in the quiet dark of the Ashen Sanctuary, the truth was perfectly preserved in glass.

Six flawless statues stood in an eternal vigil over a dead star. Paldyne and Melmori, their hands intertwined. Marche and Anna, locked in a fierce, protective embrace. Leo and Teitra, resting peacefully in each other's arms.

They would never feel the warmth of the sun again, and their true story would never be written in the archives above. But in the pristine silence of the deep, their bonds remained unbroken—the ultimate, beautiful foundation upon which the entire world above them thrived.

But utopias require power, and over the next thousand years, the High Council's greed slowly eclipsed their fear of the dark.

As the city of Orowait expanded into a towering, neon-lit metropolis, the rulers above forgot the sacred nature of the grave beneath their feet. Desperate for endless energy to fuel their pristine spires, the Council began to dig. They drove colossal, parasitic iron drills deep into the bedrock, blindly searching for the source of the ambient magic, entirely unaware they were piercing the roof of a cage.

The relentless vibrations of their machines disturbed the eternal peace of the Ashen Sanctuary. Deep in the dark, the flawless glass statues holding the quarantine line began to bear the strain. As the earth violently shifted under the drills, a single, vitrified glass pauldron cracked and separated from the shoulder of the Explorer, slowly swallowed by the shifting bedrock, carrying a trapped, screaming memory upward toward the smog.

The heroes were asleep, but the seal was beginning to bleed. And the long, neon night of the Undercity was about to begin.

Glossary

Glossary

The Nine Layers

- Layer 1 (The Endless Plains): Sunlit ocean of grass.
- Layer 2 (The Twisted Forest): A dense, damp canopy of warped trees and mutated insects.
- Layer 3 (The Cursed Mountain): A towering peak rising above the clouds, battered by blizzards.
- Layer 4 (The Dark Swamps): A humid marshland of acidic water and thick fog.
- Layer 5 (The Star-like Sands): A scorching desert where the black sand glitters like a galaxy at night.
- Layer 6 (The Crystalline Caverns): A dim maze of translucent crystals housing the elemental heart of the abyss.
- Layer 7 (The Abandoned Archipelago): A violent, churning subterranean ocean.
- Layer 8 (The Screaming Wastes): An apocalyptic graveyard of fused bone and rusted machinery.
- Layer 9 (The Ashen Sanctuary): A crater of black glass covered in crystalline ash; the final quarantine zone.

Flora & Fauna (Chimeras)

- Nighwulfs: Wolf-like pack hunters with metallic bird-legs and human eyes.
- Shadowfangs: Light-absorbing canine predators.
- Thornclaws: Massive, venomous, spine-covered reptiles.

- Insectanaughts: Iridescent beetle-bird hybrids with human eyes.
- Guardians: Headless, stone-armored behemoths with a singular yellow eye and crab pincers.
- Acid-Tails: Multi-winged mosquito chimeras dripping with corrosive slime.
- Plasmodials: Peaceful, bioluminescent aquatic slimes possessing sacrificial healing properties.
- Nurmyx: Towering, armless gelatinous beasts whose torsos split into metallic-toothed maws.
- Ancient Mechs: Colossal, rusted medieval armors animated by desert sand.
- Testanura: An amphibious nightmare fusing a frog, a stone turtle shell, and eagle wings.
- Tide-Rippers: Bipedal great white sharks with stabilizing leg-fins.

Phenomena & Magic

- Elemental Affinities: Latent, ancestral magic awakened in the descendants of the Sky Kingdom (Bolt Blade, Flood, Fire Bomb, Mind Melt).
- The Warden of the Tides (Leviathan): A divine, deep-sea cyborg entity guarding the Eighth Gate.
- The Astral Blight: The dying, parasitic star trapped at the core of the world.

www.ingramcontent.com/pod-product-compliance
Lightning Source LLC
LaVergne TN
LVHW010617100826
845148LV00014B/3000

* 9 7 9 8 9 0 4 1 7 6 3 5 8 *